Lust overpowered by love

LUST OVERPOWERED BY LOVE

Written by : Nomkhosi Nzuza

Que: Chomee wake up

Tee: Stop it I'm still sleeping

Que: You can't do this to yourself...you have to wake up and pull yourself together

Tee: (sitting up) how Que heee? Tell me how do I pull myself together when the man I have spent years with has left me for a bitch he has only known for a day?

Que: So uplan ukwenzan? Uzolala kanje kuze kube inini?

Tee: (Tears gushing down) I don't know Que. I don't know what I'll do. This is so embarrassing. Maybe I should go and start afresh in a new country.

Que: Usuyahlanyak manje!! You want to leave us as your friends, a well paying job and your family all because of a stupid man nje

Tee: Mus' ukusho njalo

Que: Ngoba?

Tee: He is not stupid Que

Que: He is stupid Tee...ayikho indoda esile engashiya a woman like you for isitshapa nje asazi izolo

Tee: You are right yaz

Que: (smiling) I'm always right

Tee: (laughing) mxm

Que: Yoh I feel like I haven't heard that laugh for years

Tee: (rolling her eyes and getting off from bed) Drama

.

.

My name is Ntando Nzuza but my friends call me Tee. I am 23 years of age. I am thick and short, light brown in complexion. I have medium brown eyes and medium long afro for hair. Lucky enough I still have indlovukazi yam uMaNzuza who is my mother and my handsome father uKhabazela. I have a few friends but my best friend is Que. If you know me you know Que. I work in this successful farm as an agronomist. I love my job and I never complain about going to work. It pays well and it has always been my dream job. I was very lucky because I got my job a few months after graduating and my life has been good ever since, well beside this imbecile leaving me for a younger girl than my life has been fair.

Chapter 2

Que: Go and bath I'll make you a good and healthy breakfast.

Tee:As long as kukhona okusanyamana nje

Que:(laughing) I don't remember asking you

Tee:(also laughing and walking away) Blah blah blah

Que

(A knock on the door)

Me: I'm coming

(Knocks again)

Me: I said I'm coming jeez

I opened the door rudely and I was greeted by this very sexy cologne. I froze for a second but came back to earth when I heard this sexy deep voice greeting me.

Guy:Good morning Miss…..Hello!!

Me: Oh snap sorry uhm, can I help you?

Guy : I'm looking for Ms Nzuza and I believe she lives here

Me : Come in

Tee:Que what's wrong I've been calling you for...OMG

Me: (clearing her throat) Tee!!!... Hello earth to Tee!

Tee: Oh ahh mmm... Hi

Guy:Hi my name is Hamilton Zungu, I am the new soil scientist at Zwane's Farm and I'm looking for Ms Nzuza. I haven't met her and I'm not sure if I'm in the right house...

Tee:Of course you are in the right house... I am Tee....I mean Ms Nzuza and I'm looking forward to working with you

Ham: Oh I only came to deliver these documents. I heard you called in sick today but I couldn't wait...these documents are just a brief description of what I found interesting about the Zwane Farm.

Tee : You could have sent an email

Ham:(smiling) We haven't met before so it would've been rude of me besides I prefer doing business face to face.

Tee: Ok at least I already know a thing about you...I made breakfast, mind joining us?

Me: Wow seyenziwe uwena futhi

Ham: Trust me I would love to but I have to rush somewhere

Tee: Ok next time than Ham

Me: (whispering) Heee seku 'Ham'

Ham: Enjoy your breakfast... Goodbye

Tee: Thank you bye

Tee:(opening her eyes and mouth wide) Mngani did you witness what I just did...Hawe mah… tall, dark, handsome and what attracts me the most about him is his cologne

Me: Jeez Tee would you please shut up

Tee:Aybo mngani kanjan nje wena awubonanga yin? Yerrr yaze yasexy indoda

Me: Tee please he's your new colleague and wena umu bingelela with a wet body wrapped only with a towel

Tee:OMG...why didn't you tell me I'm not wearing anything

Me:(rolling her eyes) I didn't notice I thought 'you were busy making breakfast'

Tee:Oh I'm sorry chomiee I was trying to impress (smiling) uHam

Me:Mxm

Tee

The following day I went to work, I knew I wasn't supposed to go for three days but I had to see that handsome guy… Days passed. I was working well with Ham and I was still enjoying his smell. I was healing from my previous heartbreak and the focus was all on me and my work.

Que: Hy girl

Me: (smiling) OMG look who's here

Que: You've been working till late these days and we haven't seen each other for three days so I thought I should bring you lunch

Me: Yoh look at the time lapho I haven't even eaten

Que: (cross)You want to starve yourself to death now

Me: I'm sorry mngani ukuthi there is a lot to do and isikhathi asikho

Que: Take your break manje and eat, I'm not ready to organise your funeral

Me: So ungiphathelen?

Que: (rolling her eyes) Your favourite dah

Me: Ngiyabonga my friend

Que: That's what friends are for, not ukuntshontshelana amadoda

Me: Lucky enough your sex mate is not my type

Que:Funny ey mxm, but Hamilton is right?

Me:(smiling) Yeah he is….ayi imah are you telling me that you and Ham are…

Que:What...no!

Mee:Kant uthini...ohhho you also have a crush on him (laughing)

Que:And I'm going to get him before you do

Me:Maybe we should bet on that

Que: R5000

Me: (laughing) oh God, before the end of this month I'll be R5000 richer

Que: Whatever...I still need to get back to work bye

Me:Bye sweetie

Hamilton

My name is Hamilton Zungu.I'm 25 years old. I'm dark in complexion and tall in height. I'm not a very fit guy but my body is good enough to get me any girl I want. I was in a relationship with some bitch and heard she was getting married with some other guy. I mean the kind of mentality this gender has. We were together for two years and I really loved that girl. After what she did I don't think true love really exists. I now deal with hoes fuck them for one night then pass to the next. I have been doing this fucking thing for about a year now and I'm really enjoying it , I mean who needs a relationship when you can get any pussy anytime. So I have been hired at this very successful farm and I must say I'm happy with everything especially with one of my colleagues who goes by the name of Tee. Yeah I call her Tee and she calls me Ham.

Tee: Did you get my email?

Me: Yep I did and I'll make sure everything is checked.

Tee: (Yawning) Well I guess I'll have to call it a day. I can't wait to get home and eat.

Me: You are hungry?

Tee: I could even eat you

Me:(smiling) mhhh eat me?

Tee: (Biting her lower lip) yeah eat you

Me: Well my apartment is close by we could drive there and I'll make you something to eat if you don't mind obviously

Tee: I really don't, let's go

By the look of things Tee was into me, if only she knew. I'll do anything to fuck her she's not my type but ke a pussy is a pussy. After fucking her I'll tell her it was a mistake and that we must keep things professional. So we drove to my apartment. I never bring bitches here I always fuck them at a hotel but this was the only way I was going to get Tee. Within 15min we were there I parked my car and Tee did the same. I got off and Tee followed me. She didn't utter a word until we got inside.

Tee: I like the way you designed your apartment

Me: I may be into agriculture but I'm good with designs too

Tee: I knew that the minute I got in

Me: So what can I make you?

Tee: A sandwich would do

Me: Have any allergies

Tee: Nope

Me: Coffee or juice

Tee: I'll have coffee

Me: Okay you can sit I'll be back in a sec

I quickly made her a sandwich and a coffee and went back to the dining room.

Me: There you go

Tee: Thank you

She ate in complete silence. I kept on looking at her

Tee: Yindaba wangbuka, am I eating too fast ?

Me: (laughing) No I'm just admiring your beauty

Tee: (blushing) Ngiyabonga

We looked at each other for a couple of seconds and I came closer, took the tray in her hand and placed it on the table and kissed her. I knew she wanted this so I took off my tie and unbuttoned my shirt. As I was trying to unzip her dress she broke the kiss.

Me: What's wrong Tee? Did I do something wrong

Tee: No

Me: So what's wrong?

Tee: Ham I'm...I'm

Me: Khuluma Tee please

Tee: I'm still a virgin.

My eyes popped out. I was definitely not expecting this. I mean I've never taken any girl's virginity. I don't even know how it feels like to fuck a virgin.

Me: Uhm we can stop if you're not ready

Tee: No I want to Ham let's do it

Me: Are you sure ?

Tee: Yes

We continued kissing.Her hands were all over me.

Me: Follow me

Tee: I'm coming. I need to put my phone on silent, I can't afford to be interrupted.

Ham: Good

Tee

I made sure my phone was recording after all, I needed that R5000 from my friend. I'm not doing this because of the money but I'm doing it because it feels right and I want to do it. I followed Ham. He was already in his boxers and the dick print was more visible. He had a huge dick if you ask me.

Ham: Are you gonna stand there forever or what

He didn't have to ask me twice. Within a second I was all over him. His lips were enough to get my pussy wet. He unzipped my dress and it was now on the floor. He made his way to my pussy with his hand. He first rubbed the lips of my pussy.

Ham:Spread your legs a bit.

I did as I was told. I had big thighs so for him to play with my clit I had to spread my legs. Meanwhile we were still standing. A moan escaped as he was playing with my pussy. I wanted the dick. I wanted to ride him. I wanted him inside me. I wanted to suck him till he cums. I couldn't hold myself any longer. I took off my heels and he took off his boxer. Shit, it came out bouncing. I pushed him towards the bed and I took off my undies. We were both left naked. I made my way to his large dick. I first played with it using my hands and then I put it in my mouth. I tried to put it all in but it was too much. I sucked him hard and licked him. I made sure I was looking at him to see if he was enjoying it. I was enjoying it, it was as if I was having a vanilla ice cream on a cone. I then went for his balls. I got them all in my mouth then gently sucked them. He was moaning and calling my name. I felt in control and that made me more horny. After that he placed me on the bed and he spread my legs apart , both of my legs were now in the air. His eyes were red and small. He gently kissed me and went down to my breasts. He sucked them and then went for my kuku. He looked at me and I was shy. He first kissed my kuku and then put his tongue in.

Me: OH HAMILTON AHHHHHH

He muffed me until my legs shook. It felt really good. After that he fucked me using his middle finger. A while after the finger fucking and the moaning he kneeled and rubbed my pussy using his thumb. I knew it was time. He rubbed the lips of my pussy using his dick and then slowly and gently entered me. The dick couldn't get in at first but after more pushing from Ham it did. It felt like my pussy was being cut in half.

Me : Ahhhhhh… Ohhhhhh… Fuck it's so painful.

It was the most painful thing I've ever felt but it also felt good. Funny right? Ham didn't stop. He kept on going in and out gently until there was complete pleasure.

Me:Ahhh Ham ahhh… fuck me babe….ahhha mhhhh oh God

He fucked me for some time and then he stopped. We were both sweating. I noticed he cummed. Luckily there was no blood. I think it's because he was gentle. He went to the bathroom and came back with a warm, wet towel. He was already clean so he wiped me and placed the towel near the bed. He then got in bed and lied next to me. My pussy was painful. I placed my head on his chest.

Ham:I love you babe

Me: I love you too babe

After a couple of minutes we kissed again. I knew it was time for another round. I positioned myself for a ride on his dick then slammed it in. It was painful at first but as I carried on it became more good. I increased the pace and the moans became louder. With him rubbing my pussy while I was riding him I felt completed.

After a few rounds, he got up, grabbed a towel and cleaned my pussy. We cuddled and within a few minutes he fell asleep. I got up, stopped the recording, dressed and went to my house. My kuku was BURNING but damn I enjoyed the fucking.

I sent Que a text that I need to see her ASAP. After a few seconds she called.

Me: Hel… (I didn't even complete my greeting)

Que : My friend are you okay? What's wrong ? Is Ayanda back? Is he trying to….

Me:Yoh Que shut up!! I'm good joh.

Que:Jeez you said you want to see me urgently.

Me:I know but I'm fine besides my kuku burning I'm fine.

Que:Mhhh umalamban' uvukile

Me:You won't say that once you know who umalambane vukad with

Que:I know you would never date any of my exes so....OMG is it Ham?

Me: Get your ass here and I'll tell you the everything

Que:I'm on my way

Me:Okay

Yoh my friend guys, une drama but I love her so much. I had a nice hot bath, shorter than I had planned because Que was already there and she was biting my head off, telling me to get out of the bathroom.

Me: Do you want to listen to the recording or you trust me?

Que: Jeez even if I didn't trust you who would want to listen to an old ass like you moaning

Me: If you say so

Que : So you really no longer a virgin

We both smiled. She's been my teacher for years that's why I know about sucking and woman on top.

Me : Yes. My virginity is gone

Que: So bekunjani? How many rounds did you guys do?

Me:(walking to the bedroom) Bekumnandi...we did three rounds… now one question at a time please.

Que: Three rounds yoh…

Me: It was too good to stop.

Que: So why the sad face pho? Do you regret giving him your virginity?

Me:It's nothing…

Que:Hlala phansi Tee and tell me what's wrong.

Me:(Sitting down) I think I've fallen for him

Que:So? There's nothing wrong about that

She has no idea what she's talking about. Falling in love is bad cause your partner will always leave you once he finds someone better. It happened to me in high school and happened again recently and since then I promised myself never to fall in love again.

Que: You are worrying me now. Tee please talk to me what's wrong why are you crying?

I didn't even notice I was crying

Me: I'm scared mngani

Que:Scared of what?

Me:That I'll love him but he won't

Que:What if he feels the same way too?

Me:What if he doesn't?

Que:There is only one way to find out

Me:(turning and facing her) No mngani I can't

Que:But why Tee

Me:What's the point? One day he'll leave me for a beautiful, two slice girl.

Que: Oh so isuka lapho lento. Just because your ex left you for a thin girl doesn't mean every guy loves a thin girl. I would do anything to have your shape. You are beautiful, smart, independent I mean that's what most men want

Me:So you think I should tell him

Que:Yes

Me: I'll think about it.

Que's sex mate called her and she left. I was not hungry so I just ate ice cream and watched a movie called GHOST SHARK. By the time the movie ended, it was already 00:55 and I was not feeling sleepy, I think it was because of the ice cream I ate. It was Friday so I didn't care. I watched another movie and after it I went to bed and tried to sleep. I kept on tossing and turning. Ham was on mind. The three words "I love you" kept playing in my mind. How could my heart betray me like this mara heee? I hardly know this guy but I've already given him my virginity.

I think I fell asleep after all the questions I had in my mind because I was woken up by a call from Que.

Que: My friend

Me: Hy

Que: Usalele aybo!

Me: I slept late haw, besides it's Saturday

Que: Any plans for today?

Me: Nope, wena?

Que: I think shopping would do after all you have R5000 to spend

Me: (smiling) Now you're talking

Que: I'll text you the details

Me: Later than

Que: Bye

Ham

I woke early in the morning to go to the gym. Tee wasn't there, I think she left yesterday after sex. I got up and all the memories came back, how she sucked me, the way she rode my dick, her tight pussy, the eye contact, her trusting me with her virginity...damn she is another thing it's a loss I only fuck a bitch once and pass on. I washed my face and wore my tracksuit. I was off to the gym. I usually start with easy exercises but today I went straight for the big weights. I felt like something was stressing me but what could it be. Mxm maybe it's just a guilt feeling, phela fucking your colleague ain't no joke. I lifted for a while and in my mind there was only one person. I kept on thinking about Tee. This is the first time I fuck a girl and think about her so much. Maybe something bad happened to her that's why, maybe I should call and check on her. No I shouldn't she'll think I've fallen for her. Have I? Mxm I finally gave up and called her. It rang a couple of times and she answered.

Tee: Hellow

How come I didn't notice she had such a sexy voice.

Tee: Ham!!

She's the only one who calls me Ham and

today it just turned me on.

Tee: If you don't talk I'll drop the call

Me: Eish Tee sorry man.

Tee: How can I help you?

Me: Straight to business that turns me on

Shit!! That came out wrong

Tee: Ngibusy yaz Ham

Me: Look I just wanted to know if we could go out for lunch today...If you have no plans obviously

Tee:Sure, why not

Me: Cool, I'll fetch you ngo 2pm

Tee: Cool

As soon as she dropped my mind came back. Shit what have I done, this was supposed to be a check up call. What's done is done. I need to go home and find something good to wear. I need to look good.

Tee

After Ham's call I called Que to reschedule the shopping to be earlier. I couldn't cancel because I had nothing to wear besides I needed Que to do my makeup. I had to look good. I think today is the day, I'll have to tell Ham about my feelings. Que and I met and shopped like we were going to Durban July and yes I did ask her for my money. I mean it's money after all. She did my makeup, chose a dress for me. It was a black bob tube dress, it was tight and showed clivage.It was above my knees in length. I wore it with a long red heel. Que did me a naked makeup and I left my hair untied. I was stunning. Ham came and fetched me. He had flowers for me, my ex never bought me flowers.

Ham: Wow...You are stunning

I couldn't help but blush

Me: Thank you.

He was wearing a black jean with a white muscle hugging golf t-shirt and a pair of white sneakers. Damn he was so hot. I stared at him for God knows how long. I was interrupted by him when he cleared his throat. He opened the car's door for me, what a gentleman bathong.

Ham:Get in

Me: Thank you

By the way he was driving a red GTI with an open top, mhhhhh I was already fucking him in my mind. And then there was this cologne of his, it made me wet...

Ham: Complement me and stop stealing glances

Me: I'm sorry... You look sexy

Ham: (Smiling) Thank you

Me: Which cologne do you use

Ham: Why? You like it ?

Me: Yes it turns me on

Ham: (laughing) I use Versace Arrows

Me: Oh ohk

We were quiet until we got where we were going. He parked underground.It was very dark, I even forgot it was 14:00. Ham closed the window. I waited for him to open the door for me, he did so and opened the back door again. He told me to get in the back, I was confused but I didn't say a word. He went to the other side and got in too.

He kissed me and I didn't stop him.

Me: But Ham

Ham: Shhhhh

We kissed for a minute or so, I was already soaking wet. He brushed my thighs, took my hand and directed it to his dick. He then went for my kuku. He lifted my dress to my waist then pushed my g-string to one side. I so wanted his huge dick inside me. I opened my legs wide without being told and he finger fucked me until I couldn't take it anymore. I cummed and tears escaped from my eyes. He turned around and took out tissues from a box of tissues behind us. He cleaned up my pussy. I dressed properly and got out of the car. He came beside me and kissed me on my forehead…

Ham: I love you

Me: I love you too…

Ham

I keep on telling her I love her. Damn this girl is driving me crazy but I'm not weak and I don't believe in true love. I'm sure she is also saying it just to satisfy me. We walked hand in hand to the restaurant. I was praying none of these bitches I've fucked showed up their face. Our day went well and the conversation was flowing.

Tee: Excuse me please I want to visit the loo.

Me: Okay than

Tee:(standing up) I'll be back

After a few seconds her phone rang. I think it was one of her friends because the number was saved as Ayanda. I ignored it but it rang again so I decided to answer it. I was greeted by a deep guy's voice.

Aya: Thanks God you answered

Wtf...it was a guy...I didn't say a word, I wanted to know who the fuck was this.

Aya: Look babe I love you… I've been trying to survive without you and I can't… I'm sorry I left you for that bitch… I know sesiside isikhathi but I can't do it anymore, I need you back in my life

I dropped the call...What the hell could be wrong with this guy(clicking his tongue) Tee is mine, Mine and mine alone.
Tee came back and I didn't bother to tell her about the call.

Tee: I'm back

Me : I think we should get going

Tee : Okay then... Are you okay?

Me: Yeah I'm good
I paid the bill and we left. I drove straight to my apartment.

Tee: Aren't you going to drop me first

Me: You'll have to spend the night by my house. After that there was complete silence.

I drove at maximum speed and we were by my apartment before we knew. We got out of the car and went to the house. She got in first and I followed. I closed the door and grabbed her by her hand. She turned and got closer and we kissed like it was nobody's business. Without breaking the kiss we walked towards the bedroom. She lied on the bed and I was on top of her. We were both breathing heavily. I kissed her neck then undressed her. I then went for her breast. I sucked them and from there I went down to her thick punani. I stared at it for a while then kissed it. I then played with her clit using my tongue.

Tee: Fuck I love it… I love it Ham

Her moans were getting louder and it was making me more horny. I fucked her with my tongue. She pushed my head in and closed her legs with my head inside sucking her clit.

Tee: Fuck me Ham please. FUCK MY PUSSY NOW!!

She was even crying. I've never seen a girl begging for a dick.
I got up and pulled her legs apart. I first rubbed the lips of her pussy using my dick then I entered her.

Tee: Oh Manzini… mhhh ahhh ohhhhhh it feels so good Sengwayo…. Ohho fuck me harder babe fuck me I'm yours

With her calling me by my clan names and telling me she's mine I got more energetic and fucked her till she cummed. I licked her punani clean and then she got on top. She rode my dick like she would never see it again until I cummed. She also sucked my dick clean and then rested on my chest.

Me: I love you Tee.

Tee: I love you too Sengwayo…

Que

Me: Tee please call me when you get this message, I'm worried sick about you.

I threw my phone on the couch. I'm in Tee's house and she is not there. I think she hasn't come back from the date but it's 9pm.

Well let me take this time and introduce myself. My name is Afika Shozi but my friends call me Que. I really don't know why. I'm also 23 years old and I have no boyfriend but instead I have a sex mate. Don't judge me please I don't have time for dating because I'm a workaholic. I work as an IT for a bank and for some millionaires. I love my job and it pays me very well. My best friend is Tee. I met her in high school. She has been my friend since grade eight. I love that bitch hey and I take her as a sister. I still have my mother uMaShozi but unfortunately my father passed away while I was in primary. My father's family moved after my father's death and we haven't been in contact ever since. I've been looking for them for three years with no luck. I believe I have a sibling I haven't met that my father made before he met my mother. I'm also still searching for him. Now that's my life…

My phone rings and it's Hamilton..

Me: Yewena Hamilton where is my friend heee?

Caller: Relax Que it's me.

Me: Why is your damn phone off? Do you know how worried I was?

Tee: I'm sorry my battery died and...

Me: Whatever... Where are you and when are you coming back?

Tee: Are you by my house?

Me: Yes

Tee: I'll be spending the night at Ham's

Me: His dick drives you insane

Tee: (laughing) It surely does

Me: Mhhh maybe I should also call Phumlani to come over.

Tee:Whatever you guys do, do not do it on my bed

Me: I'll think about that

Tee: Que please man

Me: (giggling) Bye

I dropped the call and called Phumlani. Oh by the way PhumlA is my sex mate. The phone rang twice and it was answered. That's how good my pussy is.

Phum: My day maker

His voice alone makes me shiver.

Mee: Hy Phumla… Yaz I'm in Tee's house and she is not here, would you like to keep me company?

Phum: Sure why not?

Me: Okay I'll send you the location.

Phum: Will be waiting.

He dropped and I sent him the location. I grabbed a tub of ice cream and waited for Phumlani. After a few minutes there was a knock. I looked at myself and I was fine and I opened the door.

Phum: Hey beautiful

Me: Hey love, this way please
We went to my room, yep I have my own room in
Tee's house and so does she in my house.

Phum: Your sister is not coming back right

Me: Yes we have the house to ourselves

He smiled and the action began. Mhhh he kissed me on my neck and already my velvet was buzzing. He threw me on the bed and smiled. I was biting my lower lip. He undressed and his huge dick came out. I couldn't help but smile. I love his dick. He undressed me and opened my legs. There was also a smile on his face. He didn't waste any time; he was already licking my pussy. He licked it until I couldn't take it anymore. My legs were shaking and I cummed. He cleaned my pussy using his tongue. He then kissed my forehead and then entered me. Oh god it felt so good.

Me: Mhhh… ahhh… oh baby you…you doing it... just how… just how I like it

He had no mercy...He also had that extra energy and I didn't know where that came from.

Me: Ahhh babe I'm cumming...Ahhh Phumlani

He increased the pace until my whole body was shaking. He took out his dick and I cummed. He cleaned up my pussy using a big towel that was on my bed and then he positioned me for a dog position. He was putting only the tip of the dick in and then taking it out. He did that for a couple of times and I was fed up. I wanted it all in. I wanted to feel him inside me.

Me: FUCK ME PHUMLANI NOW!!

I didn't have to repeat myself. He entered me. I could hear him breathing heavily. The pace of fucking was on another level. He had his one hand squeezing my ass and the other over my knee into my pussy. He was fucking me , squeezing my ass and playing with my punani all at the same time. I could hear him groaning.

Mhhh I liked the sound of his groan. We reached the climax at the time and I lied on the bed. My knees couldn't carry me to the bathroom. He went to the bathroom by the way I had my own en-suit. He came back with a towel soaked in warm water. He cleaned my punani using it. While wiping my pussy:

Phum: One more round nje

Me: Aaah Phumlani my pussy is burning and you are still asking for one more round

Phum: (laughing) Ok I'm sorry ke

He went to the bathroom again and rinsed the towel and then came back and we cuddled. We had this connection and I felt safe and loved around him.

Phum: So you still don't want to make our relationship official

Me: But Phum we are so happy like this, you know as sex mates

Phum: And we will be happy as a couple too

Me: You know I'm always busy… I don't have time for going out and all

Phum: I know that Afika but if we could fuck every now and than then we can date and see each other now and than… Trust me I'll understand and we will take things slow.

Me: Eish Phumlani you putting me in an awkward position

Phum: I'm sorry but I can't hold myself any longer… I love you Afika and you know that

Me: Ok ke let's give it a try

Phum: Really?

Me: Yeah but if I feel it's too much we'll have to stop

Phum: Trust me nothing will be too much… Thank you so much my love , you don't know how much this means to me

Me: Your face says it all

We continued chatting for hours. He was telling me how much he loves me. The excitement was written all over his face. He was even planning on our future and asking me how many kids I want. My boyfriend though. We slept for only two hours and I was woken up by a kiss on my cheek. I knew that was my bae and I didn't want to spoil the fun by waking up. He was leaving and as soon as I heard the door close I smiled. I walked to the toilet and my pussy was so painful. I had to even change my walk because I couldn't close my thighs. I did my business in the toilet and went back to bed. I put my phone on silent and fell asleep…

Tee

What a night!! I usually crossnight because of work but today it was because of sex and not just sex but GOOOOOD sex. I'm very tired and it was my first time sleeping at Ham's place so I have to

*make a good first impression mxm. I get up
trying my best not to wake my Ham up. I went to
his closet and took out one of his t-shirts. I wore
it and went to the bathroom. I washed my mouth
with a mouthwash, washed my face and went to
the kitchen. I wanted to make him a good
breakfast but I had limited ingredients to work
with but after all that shows he really lives alone.
I decided to make him my secret omelet. I learnt
this from my mother. I made the omelet and
boiled water to make a strong cup of coffee. We
both need it after what happened in bed while
everyone else in the country was asleep. While I
was still making coffee, Ham hugged me from
behind. OMG my burning pussy was already
asking for more.*

Ham: I see you've made yourself at home

Me: (smiling) I'm sorry if I crossed the line

Ham: Come on, this is now your house too

*When he said that I remembered that I don't know
what this is, as in; was it a relationship or what.*

Ham: Damn you look so sexy in this

Me: (blushing) Thank you

He turned me around and kissed me. He was only in his boxer and uManzini was already poking me. I love this guy and I love the way he turns me on. He picked me up and placed me on the kitchen counter. He made his way to my kuku and gently rubbed it.

Me: Oh babe mhhh

Ham: I love you Tee

Me: I love you too…

We kissed for about two minutes and I broke the kiss.

Ham: What's wrong?

Me: Nothing

Ham: Come on Tee

Me: Ok Ham it's… it's

Ham: It's what?

Me: This thing we are doing… we haven't labelled it. I don't know what to call it.

Ham: Do we really have to talk about that now

Me: Yeah Ham we have to

Ham: I love you and you love me that's what matters

I was left speechless. I know he said he loves me but why doesn't he want us to be in a relationship. Maybe he has a wife and children, maybe he doesn't love me he just says that to fuck me. I stood up and continued making breakfast. He sat down and I dished for him. I also sat down and we ate.

Ham: Mhhhhh I've had omelet before but this one takes the trophy

Me: Mh thank you

Ham: Are you ok

Me: I'm fine

We continued eating in complete silence. When we were finished I took the dishes to the sink. While I was washing them he hugged me from behind again and this time it did nothing to me. I was way too angry to be turned on by a hug.

Me: It's becoming a habit I see

Ham: I'm failing to resist

Me: As you can see I'm busy

Ham: You were busy earlier on but you managed to squeeze me in between

Me: That was earlier on now is now

Ham: What's the difference

Me: It was before you said… (and I kept quiet)

Ham: Before I said I don't want us to label our thing right

I kept quiet and did my business.

Ham: I've been in a painful relationship before. I had a girlfriend and while we were dating she got married. That killed me, from then I promised myself never to be in a relationship ever again. Since than I've been fucking with hoes. I go to clubs, meet a bitch and do a one night stand. I wanted that with you too. I had the intention to fuck you and leave you

I stopped for a second and looked at him

Ham: But after that day I couldn't let you go. I fell in love with you Tee. After years of being heartless I finally fell in love. I tried to resist at first but I couldn't. It was as if it was meant to be, it was just irresistible, you were irresistible. My heart has been tied to you ever since. But the fear is still there , the fear of loving you and you leaving me for someone better is still there.

A tear escaped from his eye. I was starting to feel guilty. Maybe I pushed him.

Ham: No need to feel guilty it's not your fault.

I guess the guilt was written all over my face and I was just speechless.

Ham: I love you Tee and I'm willing to face my fears to be with you. I can't let you go, I feel complete when I'm with you and I'm not going to break this connection we have because of some bitch nje. I love you and I want to be with you.

I didn't know what to say.

Ham: Please say something Tee please

Me: I was in a relationship and the guy I was in a relationship with left me for a younger girl who was also thinner than me. He said he deserved more than me. Those words killed my confidence, those words destroyed my self-esteem. (Tears were flowing down) I didn't see myself being in a relationship again. I told myself I'm not enough to please a man. What you said earlier on just proved I was not enough but what hurt me the most was the way I love you. The love I have for you Zungu is unconditional.

Ham: That is how I also feel for you Ntando. I really love you, look let's give it a try. Let's not let these motherfuckers detect how we live our lives.

Me: Are you ready for that?

Ham: I was ready from the first day I saw you

Me: (laughing and hitting him with the cloth) You adding spices now

Ham: I've been honest about everything a little lie wouldn't hurt

Me: Ok I'm also willing to try

Ham: Thank you Ntando, you don't know how much this means to me.

Me: Move now I must finish up

Ham: Haw not even a one round celebration

Me: Heee you should have thought about that before you fucked me for the whole freaking night

Ham: (laughing) Ey I can't get enough of you

Me: (blushing) I know hey

Ham: That's why you'll never sleep in peace

Me: Mhh I feel sorry for my kuku

Ham: (laughing out loud) You don't have to

Me: Why mara hee? Do you know how painful and burning it is right now

Ham: I'm sorry babe, you should bath and rest

Me: No Ham I should bath and go home

Ham: But I want to spend my entire day with you

Me: Ok then take me to my house, I'll pack a few clothes and we'll come back

Ham: Ok ke

Me: Let me go and take a quick shower

Ham: Can I join you?

Me: Why not…

Ham: (smiling) Mh ohk

Me: Catch me if you can

We ran into the bathroom. He helped me take off my t-shirt and we got in the shower. We were both using his towel and took turns to scrub each other's body. While rinsing the soap off he looked at me.

Me: (blushing) What?

Ham: You are so beautiful

Me: Thank you and you are also very handsome

He pinned me against the wall and we kissed. It was as if we were acting out a movie. I felt loved, special and most of all appreciated.

Ham: I love you

Me: I love you too Sengwayo.

Ham: You know that turns me on

Me: I know, I can already feel uManzini

Ham: (smiling) Shit, he has a name now

Me: Like it?

Ham: Are you joking? I love it. Actually I love anything associated with my surname

Me: I'll keep that in mind

Ham: I'm not saying use that to manipulate me

Me: I'll try not too

Ham: You are manipulative, you know that ?

Me: Ngizwa ngawe

We finished up and then went to his room or should I say our room? We applied lotion and then he gave me another t-shirt and track pants of his.

Ham: Wow you are so damn sexy

Me: I know

Ham: Maybe I should give you my wardrobe

Me: But your clothes also suit you

He was also wearing track pants and a long sleeve navy t-shirt.

Ham: Stop staring at me phela, you are turning me on.

Me: (laughing) I'll do that at work

Ham: Do that and I'll...

Me: (laughing out loud) You'll what?

Ham: Never mind, let's go.

Me: If you say so

While he was driving we were playing and talking. It was as if we had known each other for years.

Ham: Thank you

Me: For what?

Ham: For making me the happiest man alive

Me: Jeez nawe you making it sound like I've just accepted your proposal

Ham : If I did propose would you say yes?

Me: (laughing) Yes I would

Ham: I'm serious Tee

Me: (looking at him) aybo Ham we've known each other for two minutes and only dated for seconds and wena you already thinking about marriage

Ham: What's wrong with that

Me: We still need to get to know each other better and enjoy ourselves

Ham : Who said we can't do that while married

Me: Aybo Zungu you know that marriage takes the fun away in a relationship

Ham: Are you planning to leave me? Ingakho nje ungafun sishade right ? Ingoba you still planning to leave me

Me: Seriously Ham?

Ham: That's the only reason you wouldn't want to marry me

Me: I would love to marry you but not now

Ham: Why not now?

Me: Zungu akukapheli ngisho usuk sithandana

Ham: Mhhh

We were already by my house so he parked and I got out. I was annoyed by the way he behaved. I got inside the house..

Que: Look who decided to come back

Me: Let's hope you didn't have sex in my bed or else your family should start organizing your funeral

Que: Mxm

I went straight to my room and lied on my bed

Ham

Que: Why did you bring her back because it seems like she still wanted more sex

Me: Que please

Que: I was just asking

Me: Sorry I'm just not in the mood

Que: What's wrong ?

Me : I don't want to talk about it

Que : Well if you say so

Me : is my love in her room?

Que : Your love ?

Me: Yeah …. Eish I didn't want to be the one to tell you this but yeah, Ntando and I are dating

Que: Omg since when?

Me: This morning

Que : (screaming) Wow guys I'm so happy for you

Me: Thank you

Que: Wait you guys started dating this morning but there is trouble in paradise already?

Me: Sad right?

Que: Very

We sat there for a while in complete silence.

Que: Should I make you something to eat?

Me: No I'm good thank you

Que: Okay I know a comedy movie that can cheer you up, wanna watch it?

Me: Ahhm

Que: I don't know why I'm asking because I never take no for an answer

Me: (laughing) oh wow

We watched the movie and it really did cheer me up. It was the funniest comedy I've ever watched

Tee

*I could hear Que and Ham laughing out loud .
Mxm I was so irritated I even cried .
Who wouldn't mara hee? I fail to keep my man happy, I'm such an ass….. I think I fell asleep after beating myself for not being able to keep my man happy. I woke up and it was now quiet. I was even able to think. I got off the bed and went to the toilet. After that I went to open the curtain and windows so I could get fresh air. Phela Que is lazy; she only cleans her room when she's here. While opening the window I saw Ham's car…*

Me : What the fuck
I started panicking. I went out of my room
fuming. I went to the dining room and both Que
and Ham were not there..

Me : Ngyalingwa yin

Ham came into the dining room with his t- shirt
off. My legs started shaking. My heart was
already in pieces.

Ham: Babe uright?

Me : Wow Ham are you really going to ask me
that after what you did

Ham: I'm sorry babe I didn't mean to

Me : SO YOU REALLY SLEPT WITH MY SISTER
HAMILTON... HOW COULD YOU HEEE? AM I
NOT ENOUGH? COME ON HAMILTON ANSWER
ME

Ham : What are you talking about?

Me : So you are going to play fool

Ham: I honestly don't know what you talking about

Me : Mxm where is this bitch

Ham: Babe which bitch are you talking about

Me : Afika come out I know you are here

Ham: So you think I slept with Que?

Me: Ubungayekelan ngoba phela a few minutes ago you guys were busy giggling lah

Ham: You know what I won't stand for this, I'm gone.

As soon as Hamilton walked out of that door my mind came back. How could I accuse him of something like this. I went to my room's window and watched him drive off. Only then I noticed that Afika's car wasn't on the carport. I was frustrated and angry with myself. How could I be so stupid… I just leaned against the wall and slowly sat down on the floor…. I sat there thinking about how I just messed up my only chance of being happy…After a few hours I dragged myself to bed tomorrow it's a Monday and after all I have to be at work… I tossed and turned for God knows how long… In the morning I was woken up by my alarm. I first went for a jog then came back and took a shower. It was a nice hot day so I had to choose my dress wisely today. Besides the weather, I want Zungu's eyes all over me. I decided to wear a nice off shoulder red tight dress with a black pencil heel. I had braids and decided to tie them up into a neat bun. I was VERY HOT. If Zungu doesn't forgive me today I'll be 100% sure he's gay. I packed my files and made sure everything I needed was packed. I grabbed my car keys and I was ready to slay. As I made my way to my office all eyes were on me.

Me : Good morning Sthembile

Her : Morning girl… ngisho neslima ngeke sikbuz ukuthi unjan namhlanje cause it's obvious. So tell me who's the lucky guy?

Me : Aybo kahle Sisi ubani osekhulume ngamadoda lah?

Her : Yin pho eyenza u Ms Nzuza ababe kanje?

Me : Sthembile are you trying to tell me something?

Her : (laughing) aybo Ms N bengingasho kanjalo

Me : (also laughing) good ke... Bye I'll see you later.

Her : Hope I'll see the lucky guy soon

Me : Ay stop it man wena

Sthembile is the receptionist here and just like any other receptionist, she is nosey. After my little chat with Sthe, I went straight to Zungu's office to deliver a few documents. When I arrived he was busy with his laptop. I doubt he even saw me coming in.

Me : Mr Zungu

Ham : Ms Nzu... Oh my God

Me : Something wrong Sir ?

Ham : Ahm no

Me : Great, I wanted to give you these documents. They are for the new butchery deal.

After saying those few words I saw he was not listening to me. My plan was working. He was staring at me.

Me : Mr Zungu are you okay?

Ham : Please stop calling me that babe

Me : But we are at work and we have to keep things professional

Ham : Who said that

Me : It what I believe in

Ham : Well fuck with your beliefs

He stood up, made a call and said he didn't want anyone to come to his office because he was in a very important meeting. After that he locked the door and removed his tie from his neck. I was confused for a while until he came straight to me. UManzini was already up and I was also wet.

Me : But babe sikemsebenzin

Ham : Khohlwa ilokho

After he said that he kissed me in a rough kinda way. I could feel he was tense and still angry about our fight. I broke the kiss and went for his dick. I first played with it using my hand. His moans were proof that he was enjoying. My pace of the hand became faster until he cummed. I kneeled on the floor and started playing with the tipt of his dick using my tongue. I did that for a couple of times then he pushed my head in. The dick went all into my mouth. He was now fucking me in the mouth. It felt good. I think we were both enjoying that. We did it until he cummed. He stood me up and we kissed. I thought that was it cause we were at work after all but no I was wrong he pinned me on his desk. He then quickly removed files that were close. He helped me sit on the table. He first raised my dress to be above my waist and opened my legs wider. He looked at my punani and smiled. I could smell trouble. He licked his hand and rubbed my punani using the same hand. One finger then got in and soon it became two.

Me : Babe …. B..a..b…..e

The finger fucking got faster. Oh I so wanted the dick inside. I wanted uManzini inside me.

Me : Oh babe… ohhhh

I cummed. He used my g-string to wipe me. I took a breath and before I knew he was inside. Manzini was inside my pussy.

Me : Ohh babe fuck me … ahhhhhh fuck me babe

The pace was increasing and the moans were getting louder.

Ham : Dammit Ntando you so tight

Me : Mhhh ahhhh… ohhh Zungu ahhhh…It feels so good Hamilton. I love it and I love you. Fuck me babe I'm all yours.

He fucked me yezwa. It felt so good. I've never had sex this good before. He fucked me until we both reached our climax. He cleaned the both of us using my g-string and then gave it to me. There was no way I could wear that for the whole day. It smelt of sperm so I decided to put it in one of the files that were in the table without him noticing. I fixed myself and then took out my cosmetic bag to spray myself. There was complete silence so I took my things and tried to open the door but it was locked so I had no choice but to talk to him.

Me : Ham cela ungvulela

Ham : Not even a goodbye kiss first

I went to him and gave him a soft kiss on his lips. As I was trying to step back he pulled me closer and we went for a deeper kiss. He was holding my ass so tightly. UManzini besevuka again.

Me : Babe sisemsebenzini

Ham : I know love but I missed you

Me : I'm sorry sthandwa sam for everything

Ham : I've forgiven you babe

Me : Thank you love

Ham : So useza ukuzohlala nami for a few days?

Me : If you still want me to

Ham : Why wouldn't I

Me : Okay we'll do it on Friday

Ham : Why not today

Me : Haw aren't you tired already?

Ham : Hell no babe ngisangakuphinda ngamanye ama round amathathu right here, right now.

Me : Please open the door ungaze ungidlwengule

Ham : (laughing) There's nothing wrong about that

Me : Ay man Zungu

Ham : Okay, okay I'll open

He opened the door and I went out. I arrived here at 08:30 and it's already 10:30. Oh God I'm so gonna kill uHam. I went to my office and tried to work but I couldn't. I kept on thinking about the amazing sex I had just had. I closed my laptop, took my phone and went to the toilet. I texted Ham…

Me : Babe

Ham : Love

Me : I think I left my g-string there

Ham : But I gave it to you

Me : Okay I remember where I left it, no one will find it there except for you

After sending that message I got a call from Sthe telling me there is a small emergency meeting in Hamilton's office. I quickly went there and everybody else was there. Ham was looking at me in a very sexy way. You could tell he knew that under the red dress I was wearing, there was nothing.

Ham : Since we're all here I'll just get into business… We got the butchery deal

Everybody was excited. He opened one of his files to show us something… I think it's the file I put my g-string in. Luckily everyone was still surprised and happy about the deal so he's the only one who saw it and he was already sweating. He looked at me and I smiled. He showed us everything and everyone had to go back to their office and get back to business.

Ham : Ms Nzuza please stay behind I need to ask you something

I sat and patiently waited for everyone to exit.

Ham : Can we please do what we did earlier on

Me : Aybo Ham save that energy for later

With that said I got up and went straight to my office. I felt better and worked my butt off. I took my break, had my lunch and went back to doing my work. The day was very short because before I knew it was time to knock off. As I was walking to my car, I felt like someone was looking at me. I turned and I saw Ham following me. Seems like he was also knocking off.

Ham : Won't you wait for me ?

Me : Yini awuyazi yin indlela?

Ham : (laughing) Okay let me keep quiet.

Ham

Fuck I've been horny since the morning. Seeing Ntando in that dress did things to me I, myself, couldn't understand. She looked so sexy. I told Sthe to tell me when Ntando knocked off and she did. So I packed my things and also called it a day. Ntando and I met by stairs but she didn't want to wait for me.

Ham : So babe you really going to leave me?

She stopped

Tee : Shesha ke

I walked fast but since she wasn't that far I managed to reach her in less than a minute. I held her on her waist and made her turn and face me.

Me : You are so beautiful

Tee : (blushing) thank you

I kissed her and pinned her on my car

Tee : But Zungu

Me : Shhhhh

She knows very well that when she calls me by my surname uManzini really gets hard

Me : Still remember this (showing her her g-string)

Tee : How can I forget (she said smiling)

I pulled her dress up and made my way to her pussy using my hand. She was already soaking wet and that made my dick even harder. I finger fucked her using my middle finger.

Tee : Ahhh Zungu please

She moaned for a couple of times and then cummed. I licked my hand clean and she lowered her dress.

Me : My house or yours?

Tee : Ay ngeke Sengwayo save this energy for the weekend.

Me : That's not what I asked

Tee : (with teary eyes) Ok ke your house.

We got to my house and we fucked like crazy. From the way she rode my dick, you could tell she was enjoying it. I love Ntando and I want to make her my wife. I'm not saying this because of the good sex but I'm saying it because I mean it. At night we had spoken about working from home today. The next morning I took a shower and made my love breakfast. She was still sleeping and I don't blame her. I fucked that girl. I'm sure I'll only get sex after months from now. I woke her up. She didn't want to at first but in the end she got up.

Me : Sit up and eat babe

Tee : I want to first wash my face and brush my teeth.

Me : Okay ke 'mlungu' hamba

She got up mind you she was still naked. Seeing her beautiful body made me have flashbacks about the sex we had in the office, me fingering her in the parking lot and the sex we had for almost the whole night. Thinking about the way she moans and rides my dick makes me shiver. She distracted me from my daydreaming.

Tee : Awudeli neh?

Me : What do you mean

Tee : You fucked me the whole day yesterday but you still have energy to do that shit.

What the fuck. I had my dick in my hand and I was rolling the dice. There was already sperm so I decided to clean that up and spend time with my putsununu. She ate and then took a shower, only then I noticed something that made me feel guilty. She couldn't walk properly.

Me : I'm sorry babe

Tee : For?

Me : Hurting you. I shouldn't have fucked you like that.

Tee : (sobbing) Yeah Ham it is really painful, I can't even walk properly. It hurts Ham

Me : Babe I'm sorry please don't cry. (I said hugging her) Guilt was eating me man

Tee : (laughing) Shame

I was confused.

Tee : We had sex yesterday because we both wanted to. You didn't rape me. I could've said no if I didn't want to, but I didn't which means I also wanted to. I won't lie, it really hurts now but I enjoyed it so it was worth it.

Me : Really babe?

Tee: Yeah babe, now stop being a cry baby and give me something to wear.

I gave her my oversized t-shirt and she didn't wear anything underneath. I wanted to spend this day with her indoors so I had to control myself. We had a great day cooking, cleaning and playing. I was horny for the whole day but we didn't have sex.

2 months later

Phum

Me : Babe come out you've been in there for more than an hour.

Que : I'll be out in 5 min babe

Oh God she's been saying that for the past 30 minutes. We are going out on a date and akaqedi ukuzilungisa. Kanti anjan amantombazan. Well let me take this chance and briefly introduce myself.

My name is Phumlani Zondi. I am 28 years of age. I am a Doctor at Albet Luthuli Hospital. I got married at the age of 23. I loved my wife until I met this young beautiful girl called Afika. She stole my heart we started off as fuckmates but I always wanted more. Que and I are now love buddies and I don't regret any decisions I ever took about my love life.

Que : I'm done babe

Me : Wow this was worth waiting for

Que : You are bluffing me

Me : No I'm not

Que : (blushing) thank you

Me : I love you okay

Que : I love you too

Ham

Months have passed and everything is still going well between Ntando and I. The love I have for her has grown to be unconditional. She's been acting all weird these days. I think she's pregnant but I don't want to ask her .

Tee : Manzini

Me : Babe

Tee : Do you think I've gained weight

Me : Nah babe usachubby nje kamnandi

Tee : (crying) I know you saying that just to comfort me

Me : Haw my love ayikho leyonto

Tee : Stop lying ok, just tell me the truth!

Me : Okay fine you've gained ke

Tee : (crying) I knew it and I know you will soon leave me

Me : That's not true Themba lami... I'm not going anywhere.

Tee : (sniff) You promise?

Me : I promise you babe

We hugged and then kissed

Tee : (sniff) I'm horny

Me : But babe akukopheli ngisho no two hours sigcinile.

Tee : (crying) Yabonak you no longer want to have sex with me ngoba I'm becoming shapeless

Me : That's not true Ntando and you…

Tee : Look it's fine Ham, you don't have to explain yourself.

She stood up, went into the bedroom and slammed the door. Yoh this is gonna be a long road. I don't know if I should ask her or not.

After an hour she comes out from the bedroom.

Tee : Babe

Me : Ntando

She sits next to me and lays her head on my shoulder.

Tee : I'm sorry

Me : For what exactly

Tee : For overreacting earlier

Me : I think you are pregnant

Eish I didn't want to tell her but I guess she has to know.

Tee : (laughing out loud) Mina babe? Pregnant? (Laughs again) Aybo babe what makes you think that I'm pregnant?

Me : Your mood has been all over the place and usuhlez ufuna isex.

Tee : Oh so ilapho inkinga heee? You've found someone else and she's giving it to you very well mas ufika lah ususuthi usuzongitshela ukuthi ngikhulelwe. Bengingazi mina ukuthi icala ukucela isex kwindoda yakho kodwa now that I know I'll satisfy myself with a dildo.

She was fuming and I expected that but the part of being accused of cheating ay iyasinda.
She goes to the bedroom 'again' and this time she doesn't close the door. I follow her. She's crying and packing her clothes.

Me : Sthandwa sam

(Silence)

Me : Ntando look I love you. You're one of the best things that ever happened to me. I would never do something that could put our relationship at risk. Cela uhlale phansi sikhulume ndiyakucela babe.

Tee : There is nothing to talk about Zungu. When we started dating you were always all over me, fucking me in the office even in the car and now that usungidelile awusafuni sihave.

Me : (Taking off his t-shirt) Ntando if this is about sex than come let's have sex.

She screamed her lungs out and hit me with her fists on my chest.

Tee : I HATE YOU HAMILTON! I HATE YOU!

I just grabbed her and hugged her until she calmed down.

Me : I love you and I'll make sure we get over this.

Tee : I want to sleep, I'm tired.

Me : Okay babe let me remove this (I said removing her suitcase and clothes on the bed)

She lied down with puffy eyes. She looked so innocent. I love my girlfriend and I hope one day she'll agree on being my wife.

Tee : Babe

Me : Love

Tee : Please don't go. I want us to cuddle.

Me : (smiling) Okay babe

We cuddled for a while. Her ass was touching my dick and just like any guy, my dick was hard but I tried to control myself. There was complete silence until she decided to talk.

Tee : Manzini ulele?

Me : No babe uManzini uvukile.

Tee : Ay wena haw stop being naughty

Me : (laughing) Okay I'm sorry

*Tee : Babe can I please go visit my friend
tomorrow. I miss her.*

Me : Aw babe did you have to ask?

Tee : I'm respectful and you know that

Me : (rumbling) and that turns me on

Tee : What was that

Me : I said that's what I love about you

Tee : (blushing) thank you love

Me : Ngiyakuthanda yezwa

Tee : Nami ngiyakuthanda baby

Que

Everything has been going perfectly well between mina no bae. I haven't seen my friend for two weeks now, sad right? I know. We have allowed our relationships to break our powerful friendship. Ntando lives with his boyfriend and mina I don't. I do sleepovers in his house and sometimes he does. Today Phumlani took me out on a date and I really enjoyed it. I'm now cooking a simple dish for supper.

Phone rings

Phum : Babe that's your phone

Me : (running to the bedroom) Ngiyeza

My phone was on the charger so I grabbed it and took the charger out.

Me : Afika speaking hello

Caller : Haw isiphendulwa kanjalo icall yam

Me : (laughing) sorry sthandwa sam, I answered without reading the screen

Tee : No problem babe

Me : Angisakwazi uZungu usengintshontshele wena

Tee : Aybo why ungathi uPhumlani usekuntshontshile

Me : (laughing) Mxm angfani phela mina nawe, mina angintshontsheki

Tee : Phela mina ngikuphethe kahle

Me : (laughing) Ngizwa ngawe

Tee : Babe we haven't seen each other for two weeks and I miss you (sobs)

Me : (laughing) Manje uyakhala yin?

Tee : What's funny about me crying?

Me : Aybo babe uZungu ukuncisha isex yin watetema nje

Tee : You know what I knew you were never a real friend go to hell nxa. (And ends the call)

I go back to the kitchen really confused. I mean how can my best friend say what Ntando said. My heart was really broken mara ke she was expressing her true feelings about me…. I continued cooking. It was something simple so after 30 min I was done so I dished up.

Me : Babe dinner is ready

Phum : Coming

Phumlani enjoys everything I cook. He compliments each and everything I cook.

Phum : Kwaze kwanuka kamnandi

Me : I know right. Now sit down and enjoy.

Phum : You don't have to ask me twice

He sat down, said a grace and dug in.

Phum : Kwaze kwamnandi babe

Me : Mhhh

Phum : Mhla ufuna ukungidlisa cela ungiphekele lokudla

Me : Mhhh

Phum : (stops eating and looks at Afika) Next time add snakes and a few drops of paint

Me : Sure

Phum : Afika man

Me : (drops her fork out of shock) What!?

Phum : What's wrong with you? You haven't even touched your food.

Me : Nokuthi there's something wrong ngami, ngizwa ngawe.

Phum : Well it's written all over your face.

Me : Eish babe I'm sorry ukuthi nje uTee uvele wangithethisa nje and said I'm not a true friend and that broke my heart.

Phum : Bekusukelaphi eze esho njalo

Me : I was laughing at her because she was crying

Phum : Why was she crying

Me : She says she miss me

Phum : Ngenxa yalokho nje?

Me : Yes

Phum : It's either her boyfriend is abusing her and desperately needs someone to talk to or maybe she's pregnant

Me : Ntando is very responsible and I know she doesn't want a child, well not now so I think Hamilton is abusing her. Heeee Yazi uzongaz lomfana. Ucabanga ukuthi wubah yena ukuthi angasuka lah asuka khona azohlukumeza umngani wami lah nxaa.

I stood up and grabbed my car keys.

Phum : Haw babe uyaphi

Me : I need to sort out this mess

Phum : Babe it was just an opinion, no need to jump into conclusion

(Door slammed)

I couldn't just sit there and listen to Phumlani. He can't stop me from helping my friend. My friend needs me and I'm going to support her. I drove very fast. It was late so there was no traffic. I was in Ham's house before I knew. I got in there without knocking and guess what? I was greeted by Hamilton and Ntando having sex on the couch. I was so annoyed.

Tee : (opens her eyes wide) Que... You didn't tell me you were coming

Me : Anigqokeni please

Hamilton quickly walked to their bedroom and Ntando wore the clothes on the couch.

Tee : Kodwa uyaphi ungiphazamisa kwisex emnandi kanje

Me : Oh please ngizele into ebaluleke kabi lah

Tee : I'm listening

Me : Is Ham abusing you?

She just stares at me and laughs out very loudly. I was frustrated. She saw that I was getting annoyed and stopped.

Tee : Ok sorry (laughs) Ngyaxolisa but why on earth would you ask me something like that

Me : Wena why on earth would you cry out of the blue and call me a fake friend

Tee : Ey about that... I'm sorry mngani ukuthi nje these days my mood is all over the place I don't know why. Maybe it's because I haven't seen my family for a while.

Me : Or maybe you are pregnant

Tee : Nawe futhi uzongibangela iscefe ngaleyonto

Me : Ubani omunye

Tee : Its Hamilton

Me : Well you should at least consider doing a pregnancy test

Tee : For what Que because I know I'm not pregnant

Me : Phela thina asazi

Tee : And anihlangene kodwa yazin, I'll do this test just to prove you guys wrong ngoba phela nazi konke

Me : Good. I left my boyfriend alone plus nginifice nibusy seninga qhubeka, I have to go.

Tee : Kanti we were finished. Kthiwa besingakodeli besingayenza ngisho phambi kwakho

Me : Ayi bye

Tee : Bye friend and thank you for checking up on me

Me : It's only a pleasure babe.

I drove home feeling relieved. I was really worried about my friend. I just wish she could now make peace with the fact that she is pregnant. I definitely know it won't be easy for her but it is what it is.

Tee

It's early in the morning. I'm woken up by a funny smell of bacon. I ran to the toilet and puked. I rinsed my mouth and went to my bedroom. I quickly made the bed and then went downstairs.

Ham : Morning babe, breakfast is ready.

Me : Aybo Ham we can't eat that

Ham : Why? Are we fasting?

Me : No man it smells off.

He looks at me and laughs.

Ham : Babe this breakfast smells and taste good to me

Me : Than you should consider seeing a doctor because there's definitely something wrong with your senses

He laughs at me again and stands up and pulls me closer for a kiss.

Ham : The only person who should consider seeing a doctor is you

Me : Mxm I'm going upstairs to prepare for work

Ham : Okay I'll use the other bathroom ke

Me : Whatever

.

.

.

.

We are now at work and things are hectic. I haven't seen my man since the morning and I miss him but I'm very busy and I'm sure he's also busy. After working my butt off, I decided to order lunch for me and my man. I order a green salad and still water for myself and order Zungu roasted lamb and chips from our favorite restaurant. I get in his office and he is on a phone call.
I also get a phone call from Sthembile.

Me : Sthe

Sthe : Ma'am there is food delivered for you here

Me : Okay Sthe please direct the delivery guy to Mr Zungu's office

Sthe : Will do just that

Me : Thank you sweetheart.

By the time I drop, babe was also done with his call

Ham : You good?

Me : Yes babe, I'm just hungry

Ham : Sorry babe. Should I order you anything?

Before I could even answer his question, the delivery guy was here.

Guy : Good afternoon Sir , good afternoon ma'am.

We both greeted back and gave the guy cash and he went out.

Ham : (smiling)You already ordered something

Me : Yes babe ngiyazi phela when you are busy you forget that you have to eat

Ham : You are a lifesaver you that ?

Me : I know

We ate and talked. I really enjoyed being with him. He was funny and made me forget about the stress at work today for a while.

Me : Babe I really need to go back to my office now.

Ham : Okay babe and thank you for the lunch

Me : You welcome love

Ham : I love you

Me : I love you too

With that said I walked out and went back to my office. I worked and worked and before I knew it was my knock off time. Hamilton was already by my office door. He helped me pack and we went *to his car to go home. Yes since we are now living together we use one car to get to work. We drove in silence. I was feeling down. I miss my mother and I need to go visit her soon. I decided to play Celine Dion's song called Goodbye. I was facing the window and singing along with the song.*

Me : Now I know , there is no other love..

Love like a mother's,

love for her child and I know a love so complete

someday must leave, must say goodbye..

goodbye's the saddest word I'll ever hear,

goodbye is the last time I will hold you near...

someday you'll say that word and I will cry...

it will break my heart to hear you say goodbye...

I'm really stressed and sad. I want to be with my mother. I know I've disappointed them for having sex before marriage angisayiphathike eyalama allegation engibekwa wona okuba pregnant but I have to go see them. Babe disturbs me from my deep thoughts.

Ham : Want to talk about it

Me : No I'll be fine

Ham : Don't overthink, it's not good for the baby.

Me : (rolling my eyes) I have not done a pregnancy test yet Dr Zungu

Ham : (smiling) Okay I guess....

Before he even finishes his statement I get irritated by his new cologne

Me : Why did you change your cologne?

Ham : I didn't change it

Me : So why did does it smell so awful

He laughs. I get irritated when he laughs at me.

Ham : It means Sengwayo Junior doesn't like it

Me : Ham please

Ham : Okay, okay I'm sorry

I feel like I want to vomit, luckily we were already home. As soon as he parked, I ran out of the car and went to the outside sink. I did my business and then rinsed my mouth.

Ham : Babe are you okay

Me : Yeah I'm fine

We walked inside the house and we both sat down.

Ham : Babe I know we did not plan this but it is what it is love and there is no going back. Please do a pregnancy test and if the results come back negative we'll never talk about this ever again.

I was already crying. I don't know if it's because I know I'm pregnant or it's because I don't want this baby.

Me : If I'm pregnant you will not leave me ?

Ham : I won't love I promise, I love you Tee and I will never do anything to hurt you.

Me : I love you too babe

Ham : Now stop crying please, you are breaking my heart.

Me : (sobbing) ok

We kiss and one thing leads to the next. He fucked me on the couch until we both reached our climax. We clean up and shower together. Mind you, we do not use a condom. Yet I say I don't want a child and I know very well I don't prevent.

Me : Babe I'm tired, I can't cook today.

Ham : Don't worry love I'll cook

Me : But I was hoping we could order pizza, I'm sabaweling it.

Ham : Okay we will order it ke

Me : Creamy chicken flavour for me with extra cheese please

Ham : Okay love

He made the order. Within 30 minutes there was a knock. Babe went to check. It was the delivery guy. I was very hungry and I was really craving for this pizza. As soon as babe gave me my box I dug in.

Ham : Babe

Me : Mhh

Ham : Babe

Me : I'm 'misning'

My mouth was filled with bolus. I couldn't even talk properly.

Ham : Nobody will take the pizza away from you

I guess that was the way of him telling me to slow down. I wasn't embarrassed. Ham knows me naked so this was nothing.

We ate in silence. After that he stood up.

Ham : Juice?

Me : No wine please

He came back with two glasses filled with orange juice.

Me : Babe

He placed the juice on the coffee table and then looked at me

Ham : What

Me : I said I want wine

Ham : You can't have alcohol for the next 9 months

Me : So you going to control me

Ham : I won't control you but I'll do anything to protect my child

Me : Okay I was thinking of going to Adams tomorrow

He looked confused so I had to clarify it for him

Me : Adams, where my family stays

Ham : Ohho okay. Yin usukhumbula intombi endala?

Me : Yeah babe plus angikakomtsheli ukuthi inkomo zakhe azisekho esibayeni
We both laughed. I placed my glass on the table and rested my head on his shoulder.

Ham : Babe I think should respect your parents and at least pay damages since you don't want to marry me

Me : We'll talk about the whole thing when I come back, including amalobolo

Now that made him happy. He had a wide smile on his face.

Ham : So are you considering it babe ?

Me : I love you Sengwayo and I'm certain that I want to spend the rest of my life with you. Besides that I want my child to grow up in a warm environment, that's one of the things my parents taught me.

Ham : You don't know how happy I am right now

Me : (smiling) It's written all over your face

He looked at me for a while, kissed me and then I rested my head on his shoulder again but this time he pulled his arm and I was now between his arm and his body and he was also brushing my hair. He is really a blessing in my life.

.

.

.

.

Me : Noma ungathini imoto yadadweni leya Scelo

Scelo : Yah man iyona

She parked her car and came in. I walked to her and attacked her with a hug. She was glowing. I don't know if money made her glow or it was a man or maybe she was pregnant.

Me : My child unjani

Tee : I'm good mah wami unjani

Me : Angisakwazi

Tee : Hawe mah I'm sorry

Me: What matters is you are here now, but I'm confused... Aren't you going to sleep

Tee : I am mom, everything is in the car... Woza Scelo siyokhipha izinto

Scelo : Uright sisi wami?

Tee : Ngiright bhutiza wena

Scelo : Ngisharp ntwana

They hugged and walked to my daughter's car.

I am uMaNzuza. Ntando and Scelo are my children. My beautiful daughter uNtando has succeeded in life and uScelo is still doing grade 11. I am proud of my children. They are both spoilt brats but Scelo is worse. He still doesn't do his own laundry and he can't cook. While Ntando was still in school, she used to be Scelo's teacher, chef and everything you could ever think of. Scelo was basically Ntando's child and she did a perfect job. I have no doubt that she will do a good job if she is pregnant. I used to work but I no longer do. Ntando builded me a house with her first three month salary. I wouldn't have allowed that to happen and I guess she knew that's why she did it behind my back. It's been months since I last saw her and today she decided to surprise us with her visit. She is really glowing and I wonder what could be up.

Me : So much grocery Ntando

Tee : A girl has to feed her family

Baba : I think the girl has to start saving for the baby she is pregnant with

Ntando was a bit embarrassed. She faced down and greeted her father.

Tee : Sawubona baba

Baba : Unjani ndodakazi yami yolahleko

Tee : (blushing) Ngiyaphila baba

Baba : Utshele lomfana ongene esibayeni sami ukuthi ngfun inkomo zami

Ntando just kept quiet. I guess she didn't want to confirm the allegations made about her but her silence was also an answer because if they were not true, she would've denied these allegations.

Me : Ntando asambe siyekamereni, khona ingubo engifuna uyibone

She followed me to my bedroom. You could tell she was nervous and she knew there is no dress I want us to talk about this pregnancy. We got in the bedroom, I closed the door and we sat down.

Me : Mntanam(I sighed) Usumdala manje. Umdala futhi usuphumelele. Ngiyaziqhenya ngendlela oziphathe ngayo yonke leminyaka. Awungiphoxanga, njengoba ngangishilo kudala, ngisasho namanje. Mina ngeke ngiyiphathe ingane egqoka inabkeni la R2. Manje usukhulile futhi usuzokwazi ukunikeza ingane yakho impilo esezingeni.

Tee : So I didn't disappoint you

Me : Ngokukhulelwa? Cha kodwa ngiyathemba ukuthi awumithiswanga iphara

Tee : Aybo mah, he's my colleague and he earns more money than I do.

Me : Mhh let's hope angeke aze abalekeke

Tee : That's one of the reasons why I'm here

Me : Okay, khuluma

Tee : No mah, leh idinga bobabili abazali bami

Me : Let's hope it's good news

Tee : (smiling) let's hope

We walked out of the bedroom and went to the dining room. His father was sitting there and watching TV.

Me : Baba kaScelo, uNtando ucela ukukhuluma nathi

Tee

Dad turned and looked in my direction. He was not that strict and it was easy to talk to him about anything but this was not that easy .

Dad : My daughter

Me : Yebo baba

I let out a huge sigh

Me : Baba ngicela ukuqale ngixolise ngokunikela ngezinkomo zakho, ngangagcina lapho kodwa ngaphinda ngakhulelwa.

Dad : Mowungazinikezanga nje uskhotheni, umuntu ongeke akwazii ngisho nokuzikhokhela lezinkomo ngojabula

Me : Cha baba bengeke ngikwenze lokho, lomlisa engimnikezile ngisebenza naye futhi yena unesikhundla esincono kunesami

Dad : Ngabe usho lento engicabanga ukuthi uyayisho

Me : No dad, no I'd never do anything like that, besides lomfana usanda kufika emsebenzini. Ungifice sengikhona

How could dad ask me something like that.

Dad : Konconok ngane yami

Me : Manje baba lomlisa ubefisa ukuzovela, akhokhele inkomo zakho

Mom : Lilililili kwakuhle kwethu yi yi yi

Me : Mom!!

We all laughed

Dad : We first need to see that man. Angifuni ukukunikela kumuntu ozokuhlukumeza.

Me : Okay dad we can choose a day and I'll tell him

Dad : Good

We talked for a while and then I went to my room. I haven't touched my phone since I came here. I took it out of my bag. I had 7 missed calls, 3 from my man and 4 from Que. I called my man first. It rang twice and it was answered.
Ham : Babe I've been worried about you.

Me : Sorry Zungu, I know I said ngizokufonela magnifika ukuthi nje besekade ngagcina lay khaya so we were still catching up

Ham : Okay babe I understand. Unjani kodwa?

Me : I'm good babe. Cabanga ngithe ngifika nje abazali babona ukuthi ngikhulelwe

Ham : Eish babe for sure timer lakho likdinelwe

Me : Kanti lutho love they were actually calm about everything, I also told them ufuna ukuzolobola and they said they first want to meet you

Ham : Ey I'm scared babe, what if they don't like me?

Me : Babe my family is not like that, my father will be a overprotective just like any other father but ukukuthanda kona bazokuthanda

Ham : If you say so

Me : Yeah babe relax please. Don't stress yourself over nothing

Ham : Okay babe, make sure your phone is always near you, I'll call you later.

Me : Okay sthandwa sam

Ham : Ngiyakuthanda sthandwa sam

Me :(blushing) Nami ngiyakuthanda Manzini

He hung up and I went to the kitchen to help my mother prepare supper.

Wandile

Me : Hello

Her : Hello

Me : Ngicela ukubuza ngingamthola uNtando

Her : Uyena loh okhuluma naye

Me : Don't tell me awuzwa ukuthi ukhuluma nobah

Her : To be honest I'm completely lost

Me : Okay, ukhuluma noWandile

Her : Wandile…WANDILE MKHIZE!?

Me : The one and only

Tee : Hawe mah uphumaphi wena sfebe

She sounded excited and she was shouting. She knew exactly where I was so I wasn't gonna answer that.

Me : (laughing) mus ukmemeza phela

Tee : Yewena uyazi ukuthi wahamba nini, usubuya uzongitshela ukuthi angingamemezi

I was laughing really hard. I haven't seen or even talked to my friend for two years. It seems like she hasn't changed, still the crazy Ntando I know.

Me : Ukuphi babe, we have to go out

Tee : Ngise Adams girl. Ngizovakashela abazali bami lana kodwa ngiyabuya Sunday

Me : Okay sizoxoxake ukuthi sophuma nini since senginayo inumber yakho

Tee : Ungasaduka please because I'll haunt you down and murder you

Me :(laughing) Relax angiyi ndawo

Tee : Good... Girl kmele ngihambe manje, sesizokhuluma kuwhatsapp

Me : Okay love bye

My name is Wandile Lerato Mkhize. I'm 23 years old. For the past 4 years I've been overseas studying Gynaecology. While I was in high school I dated this guy called Andile and I really loved him, only to find out he was two timing me with Ntando and that's how Ntando and I met. We didn't allow that to make us enemies, instead we became friends. I think I like Ntando but I'm not sure if it's feelings or just love for a friend. I do have a boyfriend and I love him but that doesn't mean I can't have feelings for a girl. There are bisexuals and even lesbians in this century.

I've been back in South Africa for a week now and I've been living with my parents since Lindokuhle, my boyfriend was still trying to organize an apartment for me. He found one for me in La Lucia and it's my first night in it. I decide to have a nice, long, relaxing and hot bath with a glass of red wine. I won't lie, it feels so good to be back and I haven't done much but I'm already enjoying it.

Tee

It's Sunday today and I'm going back to my man. I really enjoyed being with my family but I also miss my bae… We come back from church and have a nice Sunday lunch. After lunch I go to my room to pack my things and I receive a call from bae…

Me : Sthandwa sami

Ham : Woza my love, woza my love

Me : Bambo lwami

Ham : Woza my love, woza my love

We both laughed really hard. Ham and I can be really childish sometimes.

Ham : I miss you sthandwa sami

A tear escaped from my eye. Hormones were really controlling me.

Me : I miss you too babe but I'm already packing, I will be there soon.

Ham : No need to cry babe, you'll see your baby daddy soon

Me : I love you babe

Ham : I love you too sthandwa sami. Text me mase usuka.

Me : Okay love

Ham : Ngiyakuthanda yezwa
Me : Uthandwa imina Sengwayo.

I could hear him giggling. I knew he loved it when I called him like that. I hung up and I continued packing. I went to take a nice cold shower. I was happy I was going to see my man but that doesn't mean I didn't enjoy being home with my family.

Me : Tonight I'm gonna dance for you

Owuohhho

Tonight I'm gonna dance for you

Owuohhho

Tonight I'm gonna put my body on your body

Boy I like it when you watch me

Cause tonight it's going down

I was actually singing and stripping. Trust me the way I was doing everything so good for a minute I felt like a real stripper in a club with old, rich men watching and Hamilton smiling at me. I was enjoying this until I slipped and fell. I hit my head and everything was spinning. The last thing I remember was screaming and calling my mother.

MaNzuza

Ntando has been bathing for far too long. I decided to go look for her in her room because I don't want her to drive at night. As soon as I got in her room I heard her screaming and calling me.

Tee : MAH!!!

I quickly ran to her ensuite and when I got in she was lying on the floor unconsciously.

Me : Ingane yami... BABA KASCELO!!

My cheeks were already wet because of my tears.

Me : BABA KASCELO!!

I tried lifting her alone but she was too heavy. Her father came in running with Scelo.

Scelo : What happened?

Me : Angazi nami ngimufice edindilizile lah. Scelo musa ukuma lapho, siza ingane yami.

Baba : Calm down maka Scelo she is still breathing. We just need to get her to hospital in time.

They both carried her to her bed.

Baba : Rap her with a throw and pack her clothes she will wear when they discharge her.

I did as I was told and then they carried her again. We were now going to the car.

Baba : Maka Scelo hamba phambili ukuze uzosivulela imoto.

I ran and grabbed the car keys and then opened the car.

Me : Phuthumani ukhulelwe lomuntu

They put her inside and I sat beside her and her head was on my thighs. Scelo and his father got in and he drove off. As soon as we reached the hospital, Scelo ran in and came back with three nurses and a stretcher. They put her on the stretcher and they ran in.

Me : Is she going to be okay ?

Nurse 1 : We don't know yet mah, please move aside so that we can try and help her.

Me : Please help her bantabami please.

Nurse 2 : We will mah, wena nje cela usale lah

I watched them running with my one and only daughter. I walked to his father and he held me tight

Baba : Ungakhali sthandwa sami. Our daughter is strong and I know she will survive this.

I cried for some time. I was really worried. I can't lose my first grandchild and her mother.

Me : (sobbing) I need to tell her boyfriend about this

Baba : What for? They are not even married.

Me : He is the father of Ntando's child, he deserves to know Khabazela

Baba : Uqinsile. Manje unayo yin inumber yalomfana?

Me : No but I have Afika's, I'm sure she has this guy's number.

Baba : Okay sokulinda lanake

I went to a place that was more quiet and I called Afika.

Que

It was a nice cold day and Phumlani and I decided to stay indoors all day making love.

Me : Awukahle Phumlani

Phum : Angithi you said you no longer laugh when you are being titled.

Me : (laughing) Okay I'm.. (coughing) I'm sorry

My phone rang

Phum : (laughing) Uzosindela leyo phone yakho

I took my phone and checked who was calling

Me : UMaka Ntando… ngabe ufunani?

Phum : There is only one way to find out

I answered the phone.

Me : Sawubona mah

Her : Yebo mntanami

Me : Usaphila kodwa?

She sounded down and it sounded as if she was crying

Her : Ey uNtando usesibhedlela

I jumped out of bed.

Me : Yindaba mah unani? Ingane iright?

Her : Ey angazi mntanami. Ngimfice ephansi bathroom, angazi noma ushibilikile noma uqulekile.

Me :(sobbing) Aw man manje odokotela bathini? Uzoba right? Ingane yona uzoba right?

Her : (sobbing) Angazi mntanami selokhu sihleli lah akekho oke wasitshela into ephathekayo

Me : Okay mah ngicela utshene uScelo angisendele ilocation ukuze ngizoza lapho manje.

Her : Okay mntanami ngicela uze nomkhwenyana wakhe uNtando

Me : Ngzokwenza njalo mah

I dropped the call and went straight to my closet. I took out a jean, a t-shirt and a coat.

Me : Babe I need to go, usisi wami usesibhedlela

Phum : What happened

Me : They are not sure kodwa bath bamfice elele phansi ebathroom.

Phum : I'll drive you there

Me : No need babe, ngyobona abazali bakhe and it will be weird.

Phum : Okay babe kodwa ngicela ungagijimi kakhulu, I still need you.

Me : Okay love, I'll see you later.

I took my phone and searched for Ham's number. Yes I have it, remember when Tee was doing a sleepover at Ham's and she called me using his phone, yeah I saved it that day. I called him and it only rang once and he answered.

Ham : Sthandwa sami awusafiki yini ? Do you have any idea how much I miss you... sengize ngaqhanyelwa ngicabangana nawe

Me : Ey fusegi wena uQue lo

Ham : Oh shit sorry mfethu ukuthi…

Me : Blah… I received a call from Tee's mother saying Ntando is in hospital

Ham : WHAT? WHAT HAPPENED??

Me : I don't know but I'm on my way to the hospital they are in, I'll send you the location.

Ham : Okay I'm also coming. Thank you for letting me know

Me : Sharp

My drive to the hospital was quiet and sad. I was really stressed about my sister. Ntando is a friend to me but the way we treat each other is how sisters treat each other so I'm not ready to lose her. I parked my car outside the hospital and I was just in time to hear what the doctor had to say.

Me : Mah, baba, Scelo

I said waving my hand as a sign of greeting. They all greeted me back and we listened to the doctor. We were all standing and waiting for the doctor's feedback.

Dr : Please calm down. Ms Nzuza...

Ham : San'bonani

We all greeted him back. You could see he was worried. He didn't care about being with Ntando's parents, he just wanted his future wife to be good.

Dr : As I was saying, it seems like Ms Nzuza slipped and fell. She also hit her head but I've ran some tests and everything is fine.

Mah : Singahamba siyombona?

Dr : Yebo mah ngilandeleni

Tee's doctor was a dark chocolate, tall Zulu guy with muscles. Mhh he was very sexy if you ask me. Right now, I wish I was in that bed Tee's lying on.

Mah : Oh mntanami awusavuki yin

It was like she was waiting for her mother to hold her hand because as soon as her mother held her hand, she woke up.

Tee : Ngikuphi

She said while looking around, looking for clues about the place she is in.

Ham : You are in hospital babe. While you were bathing, you slipped and fell and you hit your head but the doctor said you are okay.

Tee : And my baby, is she okay?

Ham : Doctor is the baby okay?

Dr :(confused)What baby?

Tee sat up, she already had tears in her eyes.
Tee : My baby doctor, I am pregnant

Dr : Are you sure, as in have a doctor confirmed that for you?

Tee : No but I had symptoms and my family could see.

My friend though, she was already crying. I sat on the bed and brushed her back.

Me : Ungakhali mnganami, let's hear what the doctor has to say first

Dr : Symptoms are not enough for confirmation. Sometimes you could have symptoms because you are pregnant and sometimes it could be a false alarm. I'm going to run some tests and see if there is anything on your womb.

Tee : (crying) Ngyacela bandla usheshe ngoba ngzobulalwa ikona uklinda

Dr : Khululeka Ms Nzuza I'll make sure the results are back before the end of today.

Tee : Ngiyabonga

The doctor left.

Me : Ubuwenzani wena uzushibilike mngani

Tee : (laughing) You don't want to know

Me : Aybo hawu, ngikbuze ngoba ngifuna ukwazi

Tee : (laughing) Ey girl I was singing Beyonce's song leh ethi Sit back and watch and I was imitating what she does in that music video.

Me : (laughing) As in...

Mah : Baba asihambe syothola esingakudla. Scelo silandele

I don't think they were hungry. I think they were giving us space.

Ham : Babe I really missed you

Tee : I missed you too love

He was also hugging her.

Me : Sthandwa sami awusafiki yini ? Do you have any idea how much I miss you… sengize ngaqhanyelwa ngicabangana nawe

Tee : Uyahlanya yini wena

Me : That's what your man said to me ngimfonela, ngifuna ukumtshela ukuthi usesibhedlela

Tee and I laughed out really loudly.

Ham : Did you have to bring that up

Me : (coughing) Yeah I had to tell my friend

Ham : Mxm I don't even find that funny.

After 30 minutes or so the parents came back, the doctor didn't mind us being with Ntando because she was better and the only thing that kept her here are the results. After two hours, the doctor came back and you could see from his facial expression that he didn't have good news.

Ham

**The doctor came back after some time with what I
think was the results. My heart was racing.
Ntando sat up and held my hand tight.**

Me : Are the results back doctor?

Dr : Yes, yiwo lawa engiwaphethe

Tee : And what do they say ? Is my baby fine?

Dr : Ahm, there was never a baby Ms Nzuza

Tee : What do you mean?

**Dr : As you all know, when Ms Nzuza came I only
dealt with her head but since it is my
responsibility to check for any other problems
my patients may have, I ran some tests including
a pregnancy test and it came back negative.**

Mom : Does that mean my grandchild didn't make it?

Dr : No mom. Earlier I asked Ms Nzuza if she had visited any doctor or did a home pregnancy test to confirm her pregnancy and she said no. That means she believed she was pregnant because of the pregnancy symptoms she had but that is never enough.

Tee : I could see I was pregnant dr, even my father saw that before I told him

Dr : That's what happens when a person suffers from pseudocyesis.

Mom : Mhhh kodwa ngengane yami

My girlfriend was overwhelmed and I don't blame her. You could see the disappointment and embarrassment right through her eyes.

Me : I'm sorry sthandwa sami

She wiped the tears she had in her eyes and she looked at me.

Tee : I told you guys I wasn't pregnant but you made me believe I was pregnant. Anigcinanga lapho but you also made me look forward to being a mom. Buka manje the pain you have caused me.

Me : I'm sorry sthandwa sami.

While holding her hand I kneeled down.

Me : Ngyaxolisa MaNzuza. I should have listened to you. You had all the symptoms and all I wanted you to do was to take a pregnancy test. I should have at least waited for that before anything else.

Que : Yeah babe we are sorry, besingazi.

Mom : Usamncane Ntando futhi sisaningi isikhathi sokwenza abantwana, abahlelelwe this time around

Tee : Really mom?

We all laughed and the tension broke down… Ntando was fine and we had no other reason to stay at the hospital so discharge papers were signed and we all drove to the parent's house. Ntando was in my car, Que in hers and the rest of the family was in Bab' uMkhize's car. We followed him until we reached our destination. MaNzuza dished us some leftovers from the Sunday lunch. We ate while chatting and after that we hit the road. We left Ntando's car because I didn't want to take any risks.

Me : Do you want anything to eat ?

Tee : Yeah babe, I want a double mushroom and cheese burger and also an oreo peanut butter shake from wimpy.

Me : Okay sthandwa sami

We drove to Wimpy and then drove straight home. My babe was much better about the whole baby saga. She was also playing music and singing along during the drive. I parked my car and we got inside the house.

Tee : Sekuyabanda manje

Me : Yeah babe kuyabanda but keep in mind that I have uManzini and he can make you feel like you are in a desert.

We both laughed and she hugged me.

Tee : I'm sorry Gwabini for giving you false hope.

Me : Sthandwa sami, I started the whole thing so it's my fault.

Tee : I'm just glad I didn't lose any baby, it was just not there in the first place

Me : Yeah that's better or else ngabe sifile nathi

She walked to the kitchen and dished us the takeaways we bought. We ate and took a shower together and then went straight to bed.

Tee : Are we going to go to work tomorrow?

Me : I was thinking we could work from home but if you want we can go

Tee : Asiye babe please

Me : Okay love

We made love through the night. It was slow sex that erased all the pain and hope we had about the baby.

Wandile

Today I'm going to Tee's workplace. I missed that bitch and I really think we should go out for drinks too. I asked Que to accompany me but she said she is going out with her boyfriend blah, blah, blah. To be honest, I never thought I could see Que being in a serious relationship. She always used to be the "friends with benefits" or "no strings attached" type of girl. As I was driving to Tee's workplace I got her something to eat. When I got there the receptionist gave me some difficulties but I don't tolerate shit so I was willing to go through without her permission. It's

not like she owned the place. Luckily Tee came down to take some letters written for her.

Me : Damn bicth , usungaka

She had gained a lot of weight since the last time I saw her and she was completely glowing.

Tee : Wandile hawe mah ! I'm so happy to see you

Me : Me too babe

We hugged and shared a baby kiss. If she gave me the chance I would smooch her trust me.

Tee : Let's go to my office

Me : After you

We decided to take the stairs. We were talking and catching up and I really enjoyed being with her. I even forgot about the food I bought her.

Tee : Manje ngeke ungiphe lento ekuleyo paper bag?

Me : Sorry girl, I completely forgot.

I gave her the paper bag and she took out the food.

Tee : I feel guilty yaz

Me : Why?

Tee : I'm eating and my boyfriend is not.

Me : Does he also work here?

Tee : Yes

Me : You should just open your own farming business

We both laughed.

Me : Order your man something because I won't buy food for a man who knows about oral sex and dog position.

Tee : (laughing) I forgot how you can be.

We talked a lot. We even talked about our sex life and it seemed like the girl was satisfied. We video called Que and talked about having dinner together with our men on Saturday. We concluded on having it in my apartment since I am new in it. It will be some kind of a house warming but a bit quiet and with only a few people. It was time for me to go. We bid goodbye and off I went.

Tee

After Wandile's visit I had energy and focused on my work. I think she has something for me. We have always been close but she seems to love me more than a friend. I was working really hard until a call from my man disturbed me.

Me : Babe

Ham : Babe where are you, I'm waiting for you in the parking lot.

Me : Shit! Sorry babe I didn't notice how the time has gone

Ham : Need help packing?

Me : No babe I'll be there in 5 minutes.

I hung up and packed and went to my babe's car.

Me : Sorry for keeping you waiting

Ham : No problem babe.

We shared a kiss and the flag was already up. Mxm men though. We had a light chat and today we were ot playing any music.

Me : I have to fetch my car from my parents house

Ham : Why, cause you don't need it

Me : I miss it

He parked and we walked in the house.

Ham : Why don't we go on Saturday, it will be a perfect day for your parents to know me better

Me : That would be great

Ham : Saturday it is than

I cooked a nice minced vegetable curry and rice. While I was cooking I got a WhatsApp notification. 'Wandile added you in Saturday lunch' . I completely forgot to tell uZungu about this lunch. I went to our bedroom and he was there, wrapped in only a towel and he was applying a body lotion. I held him from behind. He smelt good and fresh. I was honestly lost in his scent. I held him for a while and my hands were not resting but they were running in his chest. He turned and dropped his towel. We kissed and after a while I got down on my knees. I licked my hand and rubbed the saliva on his dick so that it could be smooth and the hand job would be easier. I gave him a nice hand job. I spit on his dick and increased the pace of the hand job. I could hear him groaning. I then licked the tip of his dick and slowly tucked his dick in my mouth.

Ham : Fuck you babe

I sucked his dick and after some time I took it out from my mouth and I went for his balls. I shoved them all in my mouth. I sucked them while giving him a hand job. The pace of the hand job increased and also the sucking rate of the balls.

Ham : Suck me babe, suck Manzini

I left the balls and went for the dick again. I tried putting it all in my mouth. I could feel it in the back of my throat. He pulled me out by my hair and he cummed.

Me : Join me for a shower.

We walked to the bathroom. He helped me take off my dress and we showered. He also fucked me like he was insane. After we both cummed, we rinsed and went to our bedroom. We applied body lotion and we both wore our gowns.

Me : Asambe syodla

Ham : Okay

We were eating and busy on our phones.

Me : Oh babe yazi ngalesikhathi ngiza kuwena ekamereni, bengithi ngzokutshela about a Saturday lunch my friends and I has planned

Ham : But babe we agreed on going to your parents house on Saturday.

Me : I know babe but I promised them before we made you and I made arrangements for Saturday.

Ham : Ayi Ntando

Me : Ngiyakucela babe, ngiyakucela Nyama Kayishi isha ngababhebhezeli.

He had a big smile on his face, he was even blushing

Ham : Wena nalama trick akho

I smiled.

Ham : Okay we can go to Adams on Sunday or even next week

Me : We'll decide that on Sunday morning.

Ham : Okay. So what do you and your friends have planned?

Me : A simple Saturday lunch with our men.

Ham : Who is going to cook?

Me : Ahm, we haven't talked about that but I know Wandile doesn't like cooking

Ham : The girl who visited you in the office today?

Me : Yes

Ham : Is the lunch by her house ?

Me : Yes

Ham : So why don't we have a braai instead

Me : A braai, why didn't we think of that… okay I'll let them know

I told my friends what my man thinks and we all agreed it was better than cooking… I cleaned the kitchen and Ham helped me wash the few dishes and we went to sleep. We were both naked, we shared a kiss and he looked at me.

Ham : I love you

Me : I love you too

I turned and he held me closer with his hard dick against my ass.

Me : Goodnight babe wami

Ham : Goodnight my love

.

.

.

This week was very fast. It the the usual, going to work, coming back and cooking oh how can I forget the great sex. So today it's Friday, my bae and I took a day off to go shopping. We are at Cotton On looking for a good summer dress with my favorite colour, yellow.

Ham : Babe buka leh

Me : Aybo babe, phela it must be a revealing dress.

He gave me a dead stare.

Me : Not too revealing phela haw

Ham : Good cause you can't show everybody my assets

Me : Isikhwele kodwa

He smiled and pulled me closer for a kiss. He gently grabbed my ass and I pulled away.

Me : Babe

Ham : (groaning) Yini

Me : Aybo Manzini asikho endlini

Ham : Should I save this energy for later?

Me : Yes

I said that while biting my lower lip… I could see the hunger right through his eyes.

Ham : Can't wait

We both smiled.

Me : Neither can I.

We continued with the shopping. I didn't only buy one dress or only just a dress but I bought almost the whole shop. We also went to Uzzi and he bought a few jeans and some golf t-shirts. My feet were burning. We went to Spur and we both ordered a mohawk combo and a virgin cranberry cosmo cocktail. After that I ordered a strawberry milkshake and we walked hand in hand to the parking lot.

.

.

Wandile

Today it's Saturday and my friends are coming over with their boyfriends. I got up early and made my boyfriend breakfast. We then took a shower together and he helped me clean the house. We agreed on meeting at 2PM so by 12:30 we took a shower again. I marinated myself and then wore my beautiful dress with sandals. It was a casual white dress and brown sandals. I was beautiful. By 14:10, Ntando and his boyfriend knocked. They both were breathtaking. Ntando was wearing this beautiful dress that was yellow in colour. It was above the knees and you could see she was feeling cool and fresh in it. Her boyfriend was wearing a black levis jean that was lightened by white and a navy muscle hugging, red golf t-shirt. A few minutes later, Que and her boyfriend also came. They were also looking good and casual. Introduction was done. The guys loaded a couple of drinks in the cooler box and went out to prepare for the braai. I was left with the ladies inside and we decided to make a few salads. Tee loves cooking and is very good at it so we left the chakalaka for her.

Que : Can you pass me that knife

I took the knife and gave it to her.

Que : Thank you

Me : So guys aniphethe njani amadodenu amasha

Tee : Girl we've been dating for months and you still considering our relationships as new

Me : Mxm izinto zay zolo lezi zenu

Que : Kungaba izinto zay zolo kodwa embheden izinto za forever

Me : And nibhalwe ebsweni ukuthi uvitamin D niwuthola day in and out.

We all laughed and Tee and I did a high five.

Me : Mina seloku ngayigcina Tuesday

I said that with a sad face.

Tee : (laughing) Yini girl, are you on strike?

They both laughed and I just looked at them.

Me : Wena mowucabanga ngongavuma istrike se sex?

Que : People change

Tee : Not us

We laughed again.

Que : Mina ngiyitholile nje before ngize lah.

Tee : Nami futhi

They both looked at me but I ignored them.

Tee : Oh sorry sesikhohliwe ukuthi nitelekile

They laughed again and I got annoyed but my heart melted and my pussy became wet when babe came in with his t-shirt in his hand showing out his abs.

Me : What happened love

Him : Eish babe ngizithele ngotshwala

Me : Ncese love, must I iron another t-shirt for you?

Him : No babe just get me another vest, vele kuyashisa

Me : Okay, I'll be back in a sec.

I came back with the vest and gave it to my man.

Him : Yabona wena

He smiled and pulled me closer.

Him : Ngizokushada

He kissed me and then walked out. He left me blushing and sabaweling for more. I went back to the girls with a big smile on my face.

Tee

The housewarming went very well. We ate a lot and drank too. I'm not an alcohol fan but today I did drink a couple of glasses of champagne. The salads were delicious and the guys almost burnt the meat. Either then that, everything went well. We all had a lot to drink so we decided we were all going to sleep at Wandile's house. Wandile has shown us our rooms but we are still sitting and chatting.

My man looks so sexy when he's drunk. Only his eyes tell the story. They become smaller and make him look like he's sleepy. I'm so horny write now I wish he could just fuck me, right here, right now.

Wah : We should have parties more often

*Que : I agree, it's a good way to destress...
Wena Tee what do you think?*

Wah : TEE!!

Me : What?

*I was so annoyed. They disturbed me from my
dream.*

Wah : Are you okay?

Me : Yeah I'm good, sorry

Wah : Okay

*Que was drinking like she had problems. She
was the drunkest among us.*

Que : I love you guys... I love all of you

Me : Yoh usuqalile

Que : So you don't love me back.

She was already in tears. Yes Que ilenhlobo esela ilile.

Que : I know nobody loves me because I lost my father at a very young age and I know nothing about love. (Takes a sip from her wine) I lost my father, I never found my bigger brother so why would you love me.(Crying) I miss my bigger brother mngani. I wish I could find him.

I sat next to her and rubbed her back.

Tee : One day you'll find him my friend

Phum : Babe asambe syolala manje.

He helped her get up and carried her in bridal style and walked to their room.

Ham : Babe I think we should also go to sleep.

I smiled.

Me : Ngyeza babe. Goodnight people

Them : Goodnight

I led Ham to our bedroom for tonight. He got in and I followed. I turned and closed the door and turned again. I was greeted by a kiss. He held me closer and really smooched me. For the first time ever, he carried me and placed me on the bed. I helped him take off his t-shirt. He walked to the door, locked and came back to me. He undressed me and I took off his belt and then unbuttoned his jeans. The kiss was deeper and I could feel the hunger in him. I broke the kiss.

Me : But babe asikho ekhaya

Ham : Luckily we have our private parts with us.

He said that and then continued kissing me.

Me : Ba....babe

Ham : Shhhhh

I could no longer control myself. I just went with the flow, it's not like there were 6 years old children in the house besides I'm sure that's what everybody in the house is currently doing.

Me : Ham… Oh Hamilton

The hunger we had for each other made us sober. We were now both naked and he was on top of me kissing me like mad. He moved from the mouth to the neck and back to the mouth again. His second and third fingers were deep inside my kuku and the thumb was rubbing my clit. My hands were around his neck and moving down to his back. My legs were tied around his legs. He was groaning loudly and calling my name.

Ham : Tell me you are mine

Me : I'm ahhh

Ham : Tell me you are mine, now!

Me : I'm yours Hamilton… Ahhhh…I'm yours and yours alone

He broke the kiss and held my legs. He opened my legs widely and then rubbed his dick against my clit. I was dying for him to enter me. I pulled the bed's cover and moaned loudly and then he gently pushed his dick in.

Me : Ham… Ham… Hamilton ahhh

He increased the pace and was now groaning louder.

Ham : You are mine… fuck

My legs shook and I squirted. He carried on fucking me until we both reached our climax.

.

.

Phum

Que really pissed me off last night so I taught her a lesson she will never forget. I really fucked her. She even squirted twice. In the morning I woke up and took a shower. This bedroom had an ensuite so it was easier. When I came back from the bathroom the bed was already made and Que wasn't there so I dressed up and went to look for her in the other rooms.

Wah : Manje ngisho nisendlin yami guys

Tee : You heard us?

Wah : The whole world heard you

Que : Yoh, I thought I was the only one who received good fucking lapho my pussy is burning and I have a terrible headache

Wah : Mina uLindo uvele wangena embheden wazumeka.

Tee and Que laughed

Wah : Hearing all the moaning and groaning I became horny and had to satisfy myself with a dildo.

Tee : (laughing) What?

Que : Ngeke uSbari udlala ngawe

Tee : Maybe useyithola somewhere else

All this time I was eavesdropping on them and after Tee said that I decided to go back to the bedroom.

Ham

I woke up in the morning and my babe wasn't there. Yesterday something I don't wanna talk about pissed me so I decided to destress by fucking my love. I feel guilty, not for fucking her besides she's my girlfriend but I wasn't supposed to fuck her that much. I'm sure her pussy is burning. She got in the bedroom with a glass of something that looked like smoothies. Her walk wasn't her usual walk, you could tell she got real fucking and that made me more guilty. I need to find another way to deal with stress.

She smiled and her beautiful teeth and dimple appeared. I could feel the body acting up but I decided to ignore it.

Tee : Usuvukile Manzini

I know I fucked her way too much yesterday but if she continues like this, I swear to God, I'll fuck her again.

Me : Yes love I'm awake

Tee : I made this for you

She handed the glass to me. I smelt it and it had a mint smell.

Tee : I added mint so that it would smell better. Drink it love it will make you feel better.

I closed my eyes and drank it all up. I don't like things that have a bad taste. I handed the glass back to her.

Me : Thanks babe

She smiled again and I felt better.

Tee : You're welcome

She kissed me and walked out. If this girl is not my soulmate, I'll haunt Jesus down and kill him again.

.

.

.

.

.

.

Lindokuhle

**They got in their cars and waved goodbye..
Wandile and I got inside the house and it now felt
empty.**

Me : It feels empty right?

Wah : Yeah ey, I wish they stayed forever.

**I haven't been myself lately and I know Wandile
has noticed but just won't ask me.**

Me : Wandile

Wah : Mh

**Me : Please take a seat, I have to tell you
something.**

She raised one eyebrow and folded her hands and laid them on her chest.

Wah : If you cheated on me or impregnated another woman, I'd rather hear those news standing.

Me : It's not that

Wah : Good

She walked towards the couch and sat down.

Me : Babe, I haven't been myself lately and I know you noticed.

Wah : How can I not notice when I only get sex once a week and only one round with condom futhi

Me : I know babe and its embarrassing

Wah : Wait, does your

She looked at my dick

Wah : does no longer work properly

Me : What ?

I laughed.

Me : No my dick is perfectly working

She sighed.

Wah : That's a relief

I chuckled and looked at her. This girl is a sex freak shame.

Me : My mother was not good. She has been in hospital for a month but now she's better.

She stood up in frustration and looked at me.

Wah : For a month Lindo and you telling me this now

I also stood up and held her hands.

Me : I know its frustrating babe but it wasn't easy.

Wah : What wasn't easy Lindo heee? Trusting your girlfriend wasn't easy?

Me : Its not that I don't trust you babe I just needed time

Wah : I don't understand, I don't know if I'm overreacting or what but I just think you don't trust me

Me : She has HIV okay

She opened her eyes wide

Wah : What?

Me : My mother recently told me that she's HIV positive

Wah : Oh my God, that's why you've been using a condom

Me : Yes and avoiding sex. I also did a HIV test and it came back negative.

Wah : Thanks God.

She sighed in relief and hugged me.

Wah : Unjani umah manje

Me : She's much better. Now that I know her status, I need to make sure she takes her treatment every day.

Wah : How are you gonna do that ?

Me : I've hired a nurse. I made her quit her job and I pay her double her usual salary.

Wah : Fair enough

Me : Yeah

Wah : We should visit your mother today, what do you think?

Me : That's a great idea, let's get ready.

We shared a kiss and we walked hand in hand to the bathroom.

.

.

.

.

Ham

MaNzuza : Nihambe kahle mkhwenyana

Mkhize : Ungakhohlwa ngifuna inkomo zami wena mfana

I smiled and drove off. Today was the formal introduction day and I think Ntando's parents like me.

Tee : Babe why are you smiling

Me : I'm happy that your parents like me

Tee : At least you no longer have the stress of having a monster in-law.

I could see that she was a bit stressed and sad

Me : Relax babe, I'm sure my mother will love you

Tee : Mhh

She was supposed to take her car today and we were supposed to be in separate cars but she said she's too tired to drive so she's going to fetch her car tomorrow. I held her right hand and kissed it.

Me : Calm down babe please. I don't want to see you stressed.

Tee : I love you Hamilton and being hated for loving you would kill me

Me : Luckily there is no one who will hate you for loving me so you don't have to die

She looked at me and smiled. I love Ntando and if my mother would make me choose between Ntando and her ey I don't know what I would do but I know I'll never leave Ntando just because my mother doesn't love her, I mean I love her and that's all that matters… We arrived safely in my apartment. I parked my car and walked inside the house.

Tee : Are we gonna order in or should I cook ?

Me : Babe you are tired, you should go and rest

Tee : So what will we order?

Me : Ahm, who said anything about ordering?

Tee : Does that mean my bae will cook for me ?
Me : Yep

Tee : Yepi

She clapped her hands and hugged me

Tee : Can't wait to eat food cooked by you. I'll sit on the couch and watch you cook.

Me : You mean, you'll sit on the couch and take some notes ?

Tee : Mina ngthathe amanote from you, mxm. I cook better than you.

Me : How do you know that because you haven't tasted my food?

We both laughed.

Tee : I just know, now let's go and freshen up so that uhubby wam ezopheka ingxabhi yakhe

Me : Imina opheka ingxabhi?

Tee : Yes

Me : Yazi ngzokbamba ngiklimaze wena

Tee : Catch me if you can

*She said that running to our bedroom and I
chased her.*

.

.

.

.

.

Tee

I was woken up by Ham brushing his hard dick on my ass. Without him telling me to, I turned to him and we shared a deep kiss. I turned and lied on my back and his fingers went to my pussy. He brushed the lips of my pussy and started to finger fuck me. He first put one finger and when I was getting used to one finger he put another one. So now his two middle fingers of one hand were deep inside my kuku. He carried on playing with my kuku and rubbing my clit without breaking the kiss. A few minutes later my legs shook and I cummed. He looked me in the eyes and kissed my forehead.

Ham : Good morning MaMshazi

I couldn't help but blush. I didn't even know he knew my clan names or maybe he googled them just like how I did when I wanted his.

Me : Morning Sengwayo

He smiled.

Ham : Slale kahle isthandwa sam?

Me : Yes babe I slept very well

He stood up and tucked in his morning shoes.

Ham : Will you join me in the shower?

Me : Yes babe but first…

I stood up and wore my gown and my sleepers.

Me : …I have to make our bed

Ham : You should consider getting a maid

Me : So that they will use muthi on you and take you away from me, ahhh never

We both laughed and Ham was in tears.

Ham : Haw babe I'm not that kind of guy

I placed the pillows on the bed and it was now made and neat.

Me : I won't take the risk love

Ham : (smiling) Ey unedrama shame

Me : Whatever I'm not changing my mind

Ham : Asambe syogeza singaze sibe late babe

He held me on my waist from behind and playfully bit my ear. We walked to the ensuite while he was still behind me holding me tightly. We walked with a penguin walk until we got in and showered together.

.

.

The day went well. When Ham and I are at work we keep everything professional. At work we are colleagues and not lovers. I don't know how we do it but we do. I cooked him a very nice dinner and made sure everything was romantic. We've been concentrating on work these past few weeks that we even forgot about ourselves. We still have sex and are not facing any problems, its just that we haven't done anything romantic for the past few weeks so today is the day I spoil him. Have I mentioned that he wrote a letter for my family asking for a date that he can come on to pay damages and lobola? Yes he did so I have to go home soon so they can start preparing. I'm so happy, just to think that I once wanted this to be a once off kinda thing makes me laugh. I never thought I would settle down at such an early age but I want to. I want to be Zungu's wife. I want to spend my entire life with him and give him as many babies as he wants. Ngyadlala after having two children, I'll start family planning.

.

.

.

.

Manzuza

My phone rings and it's my daughter.

Me : My child

Her : Hey mama how are you?

Me : I'm good mntanami

Her : Mah I know I said I'll see you guys today but ey I'm tired mama I can't come

Me : There's no problem my baby

Her : I have good news for you mommy

Me : Yini, am I going to be a granny?

I could hear her laughing over the phone

Her : No mom, the Zungu's have wrote a letter asking for

Me : Yilililililili ay ay ay ay kwakuhle kwethu

I was so happy. I don't care about the money, I only care about my child being successful and getting married to the man he loves which is also the man who broke her virginity. What more could a parent want..

Me : Ngaze ngajabula mntanami

Her : I'm also happy mom kodwa I'm nervous

Me : It's normal babe, just don't allow your nerves to take away your happiness

Her : Okay mah ngyakuzwa

Me : So when are you bringing the letter to your father ? Phela we still have to plan and we can't make the Zungu's wait for a long time

Her : If not tomorrow than it will definitely be on Wednesday

Me : Okay mntanami. Ngyabonga kakhulu ngan yam, utshele nomkhwenyana ukuthi ngithe nje ngyabonga

Her : Okay mah, bye

Me : Bye

As soon as I dropped the call, ubaba kaScelo came into the bedroom.

Him : Manje umsindo omngaka ebsuku owan?

Me : AbakwaZungu sebeyibhalile incwadi bevels usuku lokuzosibona. Skhuluma nje isisezandlen zendodakazi yakho

Baba kaScelo had a big smile on his face after I told him the news but you could see he was also worried. Its normal for a parent to be worried and overwhelmed, I mean not so long ago we couldn't sleep because of Ntando crying wanting to be breastfed and now she is getting married. I am also a bit worried but it is all overpowered by the happiness in me.

Wandile

Me : Faster babe please put it all in…. Ahhhhhh ahhhhhh ahhh

He increased the pace and it felt even better. My eyes were rolling and my whole body was shaking. I wanted to squirt but all of his dick was inside my velvet.

Me : Babe please

I was in tears and pulling the sheets.

Me : LINDOKUHLE!!!

He took his penis out of my pussy and I squirted. I was squirting for the third time today but Lindo didn't stop. We've both cummed a countless times but Lindo just doesn't want to stop. I know

I'm a sex freak but this is way too much… He turned me and made me kneel for a dog position and slowly entered me.

Lindo : Fuck Wandile losen up

I tried to loosen up by calming down… He rubbed his dick on my velvet all the way up to my anus.

Me : Ahhh Lindo

He slowly entered my anus with his middle finger while fucking my velvet with his penis. Ahh it felt good. A few minutes later he took his finger and his penis out. He spit on my anus and wetted it by spreading the saliva on my ass. He then slowly entered me with his penis on my anus. My eyes popped out and I screamed.

Me : LINDOKUHLE SHABALALA!!!

He took the dick out and I cried.

Me : Anual sex Lindokuhle, anual sex

I stood up and made my way to the ensuite and he followed me.

Lindo : I'm sorry sthandwa sami, I thought you were going to like it

Me : Ibuhlungu lento Lindokuhle and I don't like it

Lindo : I didn't know love but now I know and we are never going to try it ever again

I gave him a bad look. He came closer and kissed me on my cheek.

Lindo : I'm sorry babe I didn't mean to hurt you

Me : I can only forgive you if you are going to give me money so that my friends and I can go for a massage.

Lindo : Mxm, I don't mind paying for my girlfriend's spa treatment.

Me : You'll have to pay for me and my friends

Lindo : But babe I only fuck you, your friends have their boyf…

Before he could even finish nje I shut him up

Me : Ayke I won't forgive you

Lindo : Okay fine, I'm going to give you enough money for the three of you

Me : That would sound way better with a smile

Lindo : Khohlwa

I laughed at him. He walked towards the shower and I joined him for a shower.

Que

I woke up early, cleaned my house and made breakfast. My bae was in Capetown because of business and I missed him. He's been gone for three days but it already feels like three months.

He calls everyday but that's not enough. I want him back. He used to own three restaurants. One is here, the other two are in Capetown and Joburg. He sold the one in Joburg and now he is left with two. The restaurant in Capetown is his first restaurant. I haven't been to it but I know and have been to the one here in Durban... I'm disturbed by a notification from my phone. I jump and take my phone hoping it's Phumlani but I'm disappointed when I see its Wandile. She sent us a voice note in the girls group. In this group it's only the three of us, Wandile, Ntando and I but a minute offline, you could come back to hundreds of messages. I press play..

Wah : Hy guys get ready I want to take you out.

Me : To ??

Wah : A spa

Tee : Are you going to pay?

Wah : Yes

Me : Good

My friends and I are very rich but we also like freebies, I mean who doesn't?

Tee : Oh I forgot to tell you, I also have an announcement to make

Me : Pregnant again

Tee : No something better then that

Wah : Tell us phela

Tee : I'll tell you at the spa

Me : Why not now?

Tee : I know you guys like umgosi so I still want curiously to kill you

Wah : You are such a bitch shame

Tee : Ngzovele ngithi ngzonitshela next week phela mina

Me : Wandile apologize

Wah : Mxm let her go fuck herself, I'm not going to do that

Tee sent laughing emojis.

Me : What time are we meeting up?

Wah : I booked for 10:30, if anybody decides to be late, they are going to pay for their own treatment

Tee : Mxm nathi syasebenza sisi

Wah : But we all know you like freebies

Tee sent laughing emojis and I also did. We are all hyper but Wandile is definitely another thing…I was getting ready. I decided I'm going to wear a long cool dress and sandals. I looked at myself in the mirror and I was looking good. I took my keys and I went out. I locked the house and went to my car. U opened the car and got in. I decided to call my man before going but it went straight to voicemail.

I sighed in disappointment and drove off. I opened my GPS and drove to the place were we are meeting at. I arrived there at 9:30 because we had agreed on an hour of drinks before going for a massage. When I arrived the girls were already at the restaurant. I joined them and we ordered cocktails.

Wah : Ntando you are glowing, I'm sure Hamilton is giving it to you well.

Tee : Who said sex is the only thing that makes a girl glow

Wah : I know girl, I've been there so I'm talking from experience

They both laughed. I was quiet and thinking about Phumlani

Wah : And then wena ?

Me : Ey guys I miss my man, he didn't call last night and his phone is off. I'm worried because he has never done this before.

Tee : Maybe he's busy mngani

Wah : A man is never busy to call. If he wants to call he calls, wena nje indoda yakho isikutholele ustar

Tee : Ay man Wandile

Wandile can be really annoying sometimes but today I'll just ignore her. I won't satisfy her bullshit with any of my attention. I chose to change the topic.

Me : I saw a car like yours in the parking

Tee : Yeah it is mine, my car is back

Wah : Guys its 10:20, we better go

We called the waiter and Ntando paid for our drinks. We took our handbags and walked to the spa.

.

.

As we were being massaged we were having a light conversation with the girls. The message felt relaxing and relieving.

Tee : Guys are you ready to hear the good news I've been keeping to myself?

My eyes were closed and I was facing down so I couldn't see Tee but I could tell she had a big smile on her face.

Wah : Yes, yes, yes

Tee : Can I get a yes please

Wah : Yes please

I could also tell Wandile said that 'yes please' while rolling her eyes

Tee : Okay so last week Hamilton and his uncles wrote a letter to my family asking for a date to come and visit my family and my family agreed on meeting them on the 16th of next month

Wah : Mxm so you kept us curious for only a visit

Me : Come on Wandile this means bayokhuluma ngamalobolo and stuff

Tee : They are actually going to pay the lobola

Me : OMG mngani I'm so happy for you

Wah : Why didn't you tell us all along. Today it's the 25th, how are supposed to get attires in such a short period of time

Me : A congratulation would have been better Wandile Lerato Mkhize

Wah : I don't think Hamilton is Ntando's soulmate mara ke congrats friend

Wandile

To be honest I don't like Hamilton, actually I hate him and I have my reasons for that. After the congratulations there was complete silence. I was stressed and the massage was doing no good now. When we were done with the massage, we got up and dressed. I had to talk to Ntando about this stupid mistake she was making.

Me : Ntando can I talk to you

Her : If it's one of the the stories I usually see on TV about leaving your wallet at home, I'm sorry but I won't buy that story

Me : It's not that relax, follow me

Her : Okay

I led her to a more private place where we could talk without anybody interrupting us.

Me : I want to talk to you about the announcement you made earlier

Her : Oh you want to apologize for what you said

Me : What I said was a fact and you know. Please don't marry Hamilton.

Her : Why ehh? Why do you hate my boyfriend so much? Is he your ex?

Me : No he's not my ex but he's not good enough for you

Her : Don't just tell me he's not a good enough man, give me a solid reason why he's not good enough!!

Me : Because he's not your soulmate!!

Her : Oh then if he's not my soulmate, who is?

Me : Me damnit

Eish I didn't want to tell her like this but what's done is done.

Her : Wait, wait, wait... Uthunywe uAyanda?

Me : What the hell, no… I really love you Ntando. I went overseas to study because I thought when I came back all these feelings would be gone but…

A year escaped from my eye.

Her : So you left your family just because of the feelings you had for me?

She was really shocked and she kinda looked worried.

Me : You were always talking about Ayanda and that hurt me. When I heard you guys broke up, I'm sorry to say that I was happy. I saw a chance for us but i didn't get that chance because this Hamilton of yours had already taken you for himself.

Her : Wandile we are both girls and we both have boyfriends.

Me : I know and if you and Hamilton remain as boyfriend and girlfriend, this could work.

Her : Nothing can work lah Wandile

Me : Of course it can

Her : How?

Me : We could keep our relationship a secret. We are friends vele so nobody will suspect anything.

Her : Mxm uyahlanya wena

She said that while walking away… I stopped her by blocking her way. I stood in front of her and looked her in the eyes.

Me : At least think about what I said. I love you Ntando.

I left Tee there and walked back to where Que was.

.

.

.

.

Tee

I'm in bed with my man. He is fast asleep and I'm not. I'm tossing and turning trying to digest what Wandile said but I can't. Okay let me be honest, I also have something for her but I didn't want to accept it. I am a girl and I should only love boys right? Mxm this is very annoying, I can't be bisexual. I have to love my man and my man only besides my parents would never allow me to date a girl. Kodwa I'm lying, maybe I'm using that as an excuse because I know how supportive my parents are. Since I can't sleep, I take my phone and check all my social networks and everything is boring. It's around 2am so yeah I expected this. When I was ready to close my data, I received a WhatsApp message from Wandile. I don't know why but my heart skipped a bit. I opened the message and read it.

Wah : Hy

Me : Hy

Wah : Are busy?

Me : No I just couldn't sleep

Wah : Why?

I knew she was asking that on purpose but I answered her.

Me : I have a lot on my mind

Wah : Am I the lot of things on your mind?

Me : Kind of

Wah : I'll take that as a yes

Me : Your words not mine

Wah : Look Ntando you can try and fool yourself but you can never fool me. I know you love me. I saw it in your eyes yesterday. I saw love, hunger to be with me but at the very same time there was also fear. You love me but you are just afraid of what your family will say, what your 'hubby' will say and what the whole world will say. Mina I don't care about people. I don't care what they say because if you do wrong they talk, you do right they also talk, so I know people are never satisfied I mean even if they were I wouldn't live my life the way I don't like just because of wanting to satisfy people.

I read this message with disbelief. I didn't know that this was this obvious. I woke up, tucked in my morning shoes and wore my gown. I made my way to the kitchen, drank water and then went to the dining room to watch TV. I needed to destress so I went to the kitchen again, took out the whole ice cream tub and a spoon and went back to the dining room. I placed the ice cream tub on my thighs but it was too cold and made me shiver so I placed a cushion on my thighs and then the ice cream tub and I dug in… I read Wandile's message over and over again. It was the truth. I need to cut all ties with Wandile. If she keeps sending me texts like this, she will cause me problems in my relationship. I decided to text her back.

Me : Wandile I know I have feelings for you but I don't want to date you so I'm sure it will be better if we just cut ties.

Wah : We can't do that. We are friends Ntando and walking away won't erase what we have for each other.

Me :You are happily in love with Lindo and so am I with Hamilton. Why don't you just focus on him and let me do the same to Ham?

Wah : We are both happy in our relationships but we both know deep down there is that missing puzzle and that puzzle will be complete the day you and I start dating. We are already in love with each other so just let it be babe. Let's not try and fight what the heart wants because if we do we will never find inner peace.

Oh my God, this girl just won't give up. I wish she just stayed overseas because I don't need this. Hamilton is planning on marrying me and here I am being hit on by my friend. I don't need this, at least not now.

Wah : At least I'll give you time to think hard about this

Me : There is nothing to think about Wandile.

Wah : We both know there is.

As I was reading Wandile's last message Hamilton came in. I quickly pressed the power button and threw my phone on the other couch.

Me : Babe

Ham : Love

Me : What are you doing here, you should be asleep.

Ham : We both should be asleep but to answer your question, I was feeling cold so I noticed I was alone in bed.

Me : Ey ncese babe, I couldn't sleep so I decided to come and watch TV.

Ham : Mind if I join you?

I faked a smile.

Me : Why would I?

He sat down and placed his legs on the couch. I had no other option but to sit between his legs and carry on eating my ice-cream. I love my man and I don't want to cheat on him. He is everything I ever wanted and I don't want to jeopardize what we have.

.

.

.

3 months later

It's been 2 months since I've paid for the damages. Next week my uncles are going to finalize the lobolas and everything so Ntando is going home to prepare everything and she is going to come back after the negotiations.

Me : I miss you already

Tee : Before you know it, the negotiations will be over and I'll be back.

Me : Kodwa do you have to leave?

Tee : Yes babe I have to. You know I have to make sure when your family comes, everything must be in order.

Me : I know babe

Tee : Ungangikhumbulike kakhulu

Me : I'll try not to

Tee : Good.

Me : I love you

Tee : I love you more babe.

I pulled her closer for a kiss. Things got heated up and I could feel my dick hardening. I grabbed her ass and she moaned and then she pulled out.

Tee : Babe I really have to go

Me : Not even one round

I asked that knowing very well that the answer would be no, I mean we've been fucking for the whole night so for sure her pussy is burning.

Tee : Ayi babe haw

Me : You look tired, don't you want me to drive you home ?

Tee : No babe I'll be fine, besides I'll need my car when I'm home

Me : We don't have to use my car, we can use yours and I'll request for Uber

Tee : Okay ke if you insist

I packed her bags in the car and I drove off.

Que

Phumlani and I have been dating for a while now and everything is still going well between us. Once a month he goes to Cape Town to visit his mother. He used to do that even when we were just fuck buddies so I can't stop him now. I've asked him why he doesn't bring his mother here in Durban but he said his father's grave is in Capetown and due to that his mother prefers staying in Capetown. So he's been gone for two days. The last time I talked to him was when he called and said he arrived safely. He usually calls me every morning and every night when he's gone so this is the first time he does this. His phone is even off so I'm a bit worried. As I'm eating my breakfast, I get a message. I rush to take my phone thinking it could be Phumlani but it is Wandile saying she wants to take me out for drinks. I need something that will make me forget about Phumlani so I'm up for this. I call her and confirm the time and place. I need to prepare for my date with Wandile.

.

.

Me : Hey girl

Wah : You are always late

Me : I'm sorry, I'll pay for the drink you are currently drinking.

Wah : Now you're talking

Me : Ntando told me you guys had a little disagreement on the day of the massage

Wah : Yeah ey it's nothing that big and I'd rather not talk about it

You could see it in her eyes that whatever it is, it was worrying her so it might be bad but they don't want to tell me about it.

Me : If you say so

Wah : Yep. So how are things between you and Phumlani?

Me : Mxm loyo, I haven't seen nor talked to him for the past two days. He went to Capetown for the monthly visit he gives his mother

Wah : Is it normal for him not to talk to you when he's there?

Me : No he usually calls a lot and we also do video calling

Wah : Do you have his mother number?

Me : Uhm, no I don't

Wah : Do you at least have the location of the place he is in?

Me : Yes he posted a while back on Instagram that he was in…

I say while scrolling down on my phone

Me : Yeah nakhu

He doesn't post a lot on Instagram so it was easy to find.

Wah : Good you should consider going there and find out if he is there or what

Me : He's calling mngani

Wah : Answer phela angith that's what we wanted

Me : Hellow

Phum : Hey babe unjan

He was whispering, it was as if he is not supposed to be talking to me

Me : I'm good. Why are you whispering?

Him : Ey babe my mom is not feeling well and my full focus is on her. She is taking a nap and you don't want to disturb her that's why I'm whispering.

Me : Oh and that's why your phone has been off

Him : Yes babe I'm really sorry

Me : It's fine babe. I hope your mother will get well soon. I love you

Him : I love you too hun, bye

He drops the call first and that's unusual but I understand maybe his mother was up and calling him or something.

Wah : And then?

Me : He says his mother is not well so he's giving her his full attention

Wah : Mhhh shuthi he's under a lot of stress

Me : Yeah ey

Wah : You said you have the location of his mother's house right?

Me : Yes why?

Wah : I think you should go to Capetown and offer him your support, I'm sure he needs every support he can get

Me : Ayi Wandile I can't do that

Wah : Of course you can

Me : But I'm scared

Wah : I can go with you

Me : Really?

Wah : Yes

Me : Manje ucabanga ukuthi fanele sihambe nini?

Wah : Hawu sisi, it's up to you but it should obviously be before he comes back?

Me : (smiling) Then let's go tomorrow

Wah : Okay then we need to get a driver

Me : Okay I'll organize that

Wah : Cool then

We continued talking. Later on we ordered and also went to do a little shopping, I need to look gorgeous for Phumlani. After shopping we went to the saloon to get our hair and nails done. Although I was missing Ntando and Phumlani, Wandile made me forget about them for a while. At about 6PM we said our goodbyes and went our separate ways.

.

.

.

Wandile

Both of us were breathing heavily.

Me : Wow (breaths) that was a good one

Lindo : (Breaths) It surely was

I made Lindo a very good super and then gave him my pussy for dessert so that he could allow me to go with Que tomorrow. I hope he won't make it a big deal.

Me : Babe

Lindo : Yes

Me : Yazi Que wants to go to Capetown tomorrow and she needs my support so I was thinking I could go with her

Lindo : Why engahambi noTee

Me : Tee is busy preparing for the lobola negotiations remember?

Lindo : What is she going to do in Capetown vele?

Me : She's going to see uPhumlani because Phumlani's mother is not well

Lindo : And when did you become a doctor?

Me : Haw babe I'm just going to support my friend please

Lindo : You'll be back by?

Me : I'm not sure but a week maximum

He gave me a dead stare.

Lindo : Ufike lapha uqome, you'll see a side of me you've never seen.

Me : I promise I won't

Lindo : Good

Me : Ngiyabonga sthandwa sam

Lindo : Ngiyakuthanda yezwa

Me : Uthandwa imina babe

.

.

.

Me : Wow he built his mother a beautiful house.

Que : Just hope we are in the right house

Me : There's only one way to find out

We walk to the gate, we are answered by a lady who I think is the maid but we haven't seen her yet. She opens the gate for us using a remote control and we make our way in. We knocked and within a second there was this gorgeous woman who opened the door and directed us to come in. This lady can't be Phumlani's mother, she's too young for that and she can't be a maid, no no, the way she's dressed and the weave she has on can't be of a maid. The same woman led us to the lounge.

Lady :(smiling)Please sit down

Que : Thank you

We sat down and you could see that Que was scared. I sent her a text telling her to calm down. She read it, smiled and heavily breathed out.

Que : Uhm, my name is Afika Shozi and with me I have Wandile Mkhize who is my friend. I don't know if we are in the right house but we are looking for Phumlani Zondi.
Lady : Oh okay, you are in the right house. My name is Anelisa, I'm Phuml

Phum : Honey I'm home

I looked at Que confused. How the hell did Phumlani know that Afika is here, I thought it was going to be a surprise. Anelisa stood up.

Lisa : Please excuse me for a sec

She walked to where Phumlani was.

Me : Que??

Que : I'm just as confused as you are.

Lisa

Me : Hy babe you have visitors

Phum : Who? Me?

Me : Of course you haw

We walked to the lounge and Phumlani's eyes just popped out when he saw his visitors.

Ham

Since Ntando went to the farm, I decided to go to her apartment. I might get something to prove if what I'm thinking is true or not. So now I'm driving to Tee's apartment and I'm praying I don't find Que there. It would be even worse if I was to find her with or having sex with Phumlani. My phone rings and it's the love of my life.

Me : Sthandwa sami

You could tell she was blushing

Tee : Babe wami

I also couldn't help but smile.

Me : How are you

Tee : I miss you

Me : I also miss you babe but we had to do things the right way

Tee : Yeah I understand

Me : Look babe I'm driving, I'm going to buy something to eat so when I get home I'll video call you
Tee : Okay sthandwa sam, I love you

Me : I love you too

She giggled and then dropped. She can be another thing yaz. She's not an expensive woman that needs to be pleased with expensive jewellery or expensive dates. She's just a simple girlfriend that buys herself what she wants and is satisfied by the little things you offer, priceless things like time and attention. Damn how can I forget very good sex. If you give her these few things she respects you and knows you are the man.

After some time I got to Tee's apartment. I talk to the security, give him a few bucks and he let's me go through. I get in the apartment, walk around to make sure nobody is here and I'm relieved because nobody was here. I make my way to Afika's room. When I get there I look everywhere for something I could use but I find nothing. After that I went to her ensuite and I find a toothbrush. Bingo I think it's her's so I take it and make my way out making sure I leave everything the way I found it.

Lisa

Me : Sthandwa sami are you okay?

So now the visitor's eyes popped out. I was so annoyed and confused.

Me : Can somebody please tell me what the fuck is going on

Wandile stood up and looked me straight in the eyes.

Wah : You want to know what the fuck is happening

Me : Ofcourse

Wah : Well I'll tell you

She said that moving her eyes to Phumlani's eyes.

Que : Wandile please let's go

Wah : I'm not going anywhere. This so-called husband of yours cheating on you with Que. We knew nothing about you and we thought he came to his mother here.

After the word cheating, I heard nothing. Tears were flowing down my eyes. I love Phumlani so much and hearing that he is cheating on me just breaks my heart. Ntwenhle came downstairs and my heart broke even more. I don't like crying in front of her.

Ntwenhle : Mommy are you okay? Daddy why is mommy crying?

Worry was written all over her face. I went to her and kneeled down so I could be the same height as her.

Me : Mommy will be fine baby okay?

She nodded.

Me : Now go back upstairs baby.

Enhle : If I go back upstairs we you stop crying

Me : Yes baby I'll stop

I said that wiping my tears

Enhle : I love you mommy

Me : I love you too my Angel.

I hugged her and then she went back upstairs.

Que : So you even have a child, wow!

Que grabbed her bag, looked at Phumlani with disgust.

Que : Nxa, uyanginyanyisa. Chommie asambe.

They walked out and slammed the door.

Ham

So today is the day, when the sunset Ntando will traditionally be my wife. I don't want to lie, I am very scared. Ntando and I spent the whole of last night talking over the phone trying to calm each other's nerves down but the fear is still there. Maybe Mr Mkhize has changed his mind about allowing me to marry his daughter, maybe they'll demand more than what we talked about on the day of the damages, maybe Ntando changed her mind. Yoh, yoh, I'm scared and I can see all of this thinking will drive me crazy.

So we are on our way to eMzinto, where Ntando's farm is. That is where everything will take place. I'll obviously be sitting in the car while my uncles and Ntando's uncles negotiate. We've finally reached our destination and I am sweating. We have cows with us and they are alive and strong. They did cost me a fortune but I don't mind. Money is really nothing compared to the person I'll get in return. My uncles leave me in the car and make their way towards the house. They stop by the gate and shout the Nzuza clan names and beg to be let in.

Tee

I was in the kitchen helping with the final touches when I heard a man shouting from the gate. Oh my God. The last time I talked to Hamilton they were 30 minutes away and that was only a few minutes ago, well as far as I know it was a few minutes ago. I was really scared. My uncles can be overprotective sometimes and they can demand stupid things just to 'give me more time to think' well that's what they say.

Man 1 : Nina boMshazi, nina boMahlobo sicela nisingenise kwikhaya lenu. Syacela boNzuza, Debelimdaka, Wena owahlaba iso leso ngomusa wahlaba elengonyama. Sivuleleni Nozishada kaMaqhoboza.

Yoh that guy was really screaming his lungs out. My uncles sent Scelo to go to the gate and open for the Zungu men. My mother came into the kitchen while I was peeping and directed me to my room. Apparently the groom's family can't see me before they pay the lobola. So I came out of the hut that was the kitchen and made my way to the bid house where my room was.
Me : Oh well done mama, now I can't see anything.

Mom : Isiko, isiko mntanam.

Me : I'm really scared mom

Mom : It's normal, I was also as scared as you are when ubaba wakho sent his uncles to my house to pay the lobola.

Me : Ey mah, you know how uncle Nhlanhla can be. He'll just make things hard for Zungu.

Mom : He should mntanam. You are special. You are young, you were well raised, you are smart and successful. Zungu also knows that you will cost him a fortune. Besides all of this he's the one who took your virginity and for that he should really pay.

Me : He said he has 20 cows with him

My mother's eyes popped out. She was shocked.

Mom : 20? 20 cows Ntando?
Me : Please don't tell me they are not enough.

Mom : Aybo they are more than enough. That Zungu man really loves you and he sees the potential you have or else he wouldn't have agreed to so much.

With that said, I smiled and my nerves were calmed.

Wandile and Afika came in. They've been here since Thursday and by the way today it's Saturday. They've been very supportive and without their support maybe I would have been in hospital because of stress.

Wah : Guys asambe syogeza sibe bahle.

Me : Ay guys I'll bathe after the negotiations.

Wah : Are you crazy, are you seriously going to see your husband and your in-laws covered by beetroot and curry stains?

Mom : Hamba Nana

Me : Okay fine who will start?

Wah : Let's shower together

Oh God, my childish friends

Que : That sounds fun asambe

I just rolled my eyes and followed them to the bathroom. I really didn't have any energy to argue with them. We showered together, Wandile did our makeup and then we got dressed in our traditional attires.

Somebody knocked once and opened. My heart skipped a beat. It was Scelo. He just popped his head in and the rest of his body remained outside.

Scelo : Mah uthe ubaba lungisa osisi sekufanele kukhethwe umakoti

Mah : Okay my son

With that said he turned back and pulled the door.
Me : Does that mean the negotiations are over

Mah : Yes, the major and most important part is over.

I sighed out of relief.

Mah : Hurry up girls we have to go to the kitchen to see if your in-laws know who their makoti is.

Que : But friend you've only seen them once or twice, will they be able to identify you ?

Me : (whispering) I gave Hamilton a hint and he told them, well I hope he told them.

Mah : That's what we all did so there is no need to whisper.

We all laughed… My mother neatly covered our hair with a scarf and we walked to the hut where the negotiations were held. We had to kneel down and face the floor. We were not allowed to look the men straight into their eyes, apparently looking men in their eyes was a sign of disrespect. One of Hamilton's uncle made his way towards us. I was not sure which one because I was facing down. I was in the middle and I had told Hamilton that I will be wearing a navy blue scarf so that was the way they were going to spot me. The uncle touched me on my head.

Uncle : Uye loh umakoti wethu

I smiled and felt relieved.

I could hear my mother ulululating and that was a good sign. I think everything went accordingly. Scelo was sent to go call Ham from the car… After two minutes or so he came back with him. I couldn't hold myself so I stole a glance and smiled. I became horny the moment I saw him. Don't blame me it's been a week since I last saw my man. He was so sexy. Oh and his cologne. It felt like it was the first I ever smelt it. It made me fall in love with him all over again.

We did everything we were supposed to do. I had to even give my men and my in-laws a basin to wash their hands while kneeling before I served them and again I had to kneel when I served them. I swear to God, by the time all of this is over, I'll be paralyzed. Ham and I had matching traditional attires but we were not wearing them because I recently bought them and they are in my room. I wanted us to wear them so I first asked for permission from my mother and she agreed after giving me a deadly stare… I told my husband oh yes my Husband, and he followed me to my room. I closed and locked the door and yeah we couldn't act like 2 year olds.

Ham : Waze wamuhle mnkami

He said that coming towards me. I couldn't help but blush. The hunger he had for me was written all over his face. He got closer and we kissed. It wasn't a slow and passionate kiss but it was a 'we only have a few minutes' kinda kiss. He ripped off my dress and I helped him take off his top. We were breathing heavily. He grabbed me on my butt and I hugged him with my legs. He was now carrying me.

Ham : I love you MaZungu, I love you so much.

Me : I love you too mnyeni wami
It was like I added fuel to fire. He was very hard. He unzipped his pants and took out his dick mean while he was still carrying me and my legs were still wrapped around him. He brushed my pussy.

Me : Ohhhh baby

He slightly made his way in with his dick. I covered my mouth and moaned.

Me : Mhhhh

And then there was a knock. We both popped our eyes out and there was a voice.

Voice : Sisi uyakucela umah ezansi

I rolled my eyes. I was so pissed, it was Scelo.

Me : Okay I'm coming.

I gave Zungu a baby kiss.

Me : I'm sorry sthandwa sami

Ham : It's fine babe, we were not supposed to do this anyway.

I unwrapped my legs and showed him what he was going to wear. He smiled.

Ham : Wow

Me : You like?

Ham : Definitely

We wore our matching attires and we looked good in them.

Ham : You are so beautiful

Me : And you are so handsome

He came closer and now we shared a kiss. This time it was more slow and passionate. After some time he broke the kiss.

Ham : Let's go before your mother comes here.

I laughed and we walked out. He made his way to the other men and I went to Que. I know my mother called me but I know my mother, she was telling me to get out and not do any silly things.

Que : You should have stayed in your room for a few minutes, just to calm down and wipe the hunger written in your eyes.

Tee : Is it that obvious?

Que : If I could see it, it means it is obvious.

Tee : Were is Wandile, maybe she can fix my make up.

Que : She's in her room, probably fucking with Lindo.

Tee : Oh Lindo came?

Que : Yes

Tee : Wow, okay.

Que : Maybe I should get myself Hamilton's uncle.

Oh there was this uncle of Ham that was very good looking. I think he is the youngest. He has a nice, fit and sexy body but you could also see that he was not matured because he looked like a player.

Tee : Hold your horses

Que : Kodwa mngani

Tee : Ayi Que, not here and definitely not today

Que : Okay ke boring mosadi

Tee : Whatever.

Wah

Me : Do you really have to go

Lindo : Yes Wandile, having sex here was a sign of disrespect, I can't do anymore wrong.

Me : Okay ke
Lindo : I love you

Me : I love you too.

We shared a long kiss and after that he zipped my dress and I accompanied him to his car.

Lindo : Yazi I haven't seen Ntando or Hamilton just to congratulate them and let them know I was also here to support them.

Me : Well I don't know were... oh there they are.

They were walking towards us.

Ham : Bafo

Lindo : Mf'wethu

They shook hands.

Lindo : Ngyakubongela bafo, you are a real man.

Ham : Kubonga mina zalo

Lindo : MaZungu
Ntando blushed and looked at Lindo.

Tee : Yebo Lindo

Lindo : Congrats my sister

They shared a friendly hug.

Lindo : I got you guys a little something but it's in the car.

Me : I'll come back with it

Lindo : Okay than. People I need to leave now. I had a great time and the food was really amazing. Unfortunately I couldn't drink alcohol because I still have to drive.

Ham : Khululeka, when I see you again, I'll buy you a bottle of whiskey.

Lindo : Now that's closure

We all laughed.

Lindo : Goodbye guys
Ham : Uhambe kahle bafo and thank you for the support.

Lindo : Anytime

We walked to the car. He's still here but I already miss him.